W9-CAX-358

places, and incidents either are products of the author's imagination or are used fictitiously. Any resemblance to actual

lisher of this work. The author is deeply grateful to the Bogliasco Foundation for its generous support. Book design by Chip Kidd, who wrote it in Quark 3.2. Text is set in Apollo and then, at a certain point, Bodoni. Cheese Monkeys logo designed by Mr. F. C. Ware.   Manufactured in the United States of America. 1 3 5 7 9 10 8 6 4 2 • Library

of Congress Cataloging-in-Publication Data available. ISBN 0-7432-1492-7. And now,

CHEESE MO

A NOVEL *in* TWO

BY

CHIP

SCRIBNER

KEYS.

SEMESTERS

KIDD.

NEW YORK LONDON TORONTO SYDNEY SINGAPORE

For L.S., B.K., and S.C.

CONT.

_____

XV   PRELUDE

FALL SEMESTER, 1957

2   i.   REGISTRATION

21   ii. ART 101: INTRODUCTION TO DRAWING.

57   iii. ART 101: INTRODUCTION TO DRAWING. (cont'd)

85   iv. WINTER BREAK

SPRING SEMESTER, 1958

96   i.   ART 127: INTRODUCTION TO COMMERCIAL ART.

115   ii. THE FIRST CRITIQUE.

149   iii. THE SECOND CRITIQUE.

173   iv. THE THIRD CRITIQUE.

213   v.   THE FOURTH CRITIQUE.

266   vi. THE FINAL EXAM.

"God is great. God is good. Let us thank him for this food."

—trad. Am. prayer

"America is great because America is good."

—Alexis de Tocqueville, *Democracy in America*

"Good is dead."

— W. Sorbeck

1 9 5 8

"Ladies and Gentlemen, behold: The Enemy:"

He raised the blinds, and there was the street below. Townies going up and down upon the land. Greased, efficient gears in the Village engine. Harmless.

"Relentless. Unstoppable. You cannot hope to defeat them. Nor, as a matter of fact, would you want to. Their defeat also means yours. When a host dies, he takes his virus with him. Viruses are fools—they work toward their own extinction. Not you. You will sustain the enemy as long as possible, and flourish.

"So why are they the enemy? Because they are bent on destroying you. They did it yesterday. They'll do it tomorrow. They're curing themselves of you as I speak—their serum is Indifference. Your job is to infect them, to elude the antidote, and to thrive. To make your thoughts into their obsessions, your whims into their rapacious desires. And I will show you how to do it. If this isn't what you had in mind, leave now to join them and become our food and save me considerable trouble. My job is to give you courage, cunning, power. To make you strong. To make you smarter. To make you ruthless. Because when you leave here, you are not just going to work.

"You are going to war."

FALL SEMESTER

1957

REGISTRATION

During which we construct our course of study.

"So, what are you taking?"

At that point I could have said a lot of things—I could have said, "If I don't get the classes I need after waiting five hours in this line, I am taking that clipboard out of your sausage-fingered hands, breaking it into ten thick splinters, and slowly introducing each one of them beneath your cuticles as a way of saying Thanks for herding us like a flock of three thousand Guatemalan dirt pigs into a ventilation-free hall built for three hundred in order to ask us questions we've already answered so many times our minds are jelly and our jaws squeak—an act which *has* to be covered somewhere in the Bible as punishable by any manner we, in His righteous stead, see fit."

But I didn't.

I mumbled for the umpteenth time that year-long day of that first awful month, my tongue thick with shame,

"Me? Art."

• • •

Majoring in Art at the state university appealed to me because I have always hated Art, and I had a hunch if any school would treat the subject with the proper disdain, it would be one that was run by the government. Of course I was right. My suspicions were confirmed the minute I entered the Visual Arts building on arrival my freshmen year and took in the faculty show in its gallery. I beheld: melting lop-sided Umbrian? hillsides, nudes run over by the Cubist Express, suburban-surrealist flower ladies going about their daily tasks weeping blood tears the size of water balloons, and kittens. Yes, kittens. I thought, "Now *these* people hate Art *a lot. This* is where I belong. Perfect."

So what *did* I like? Well, that spring of senior year at Upper Wissahicken High I was quite pleased with a drawing in green pencil I did on the margin of a page in my dreary Civics textbook of Mickey Mouse (from the Steamboat Willy era— when he really looked like something you'd set out a trap for and cross your fingers) ritually eviscerating Olive Oyl with an oyster fork, because it marked the first time I finally got the proportion of his eyes to his mouth and nose absolutely right without any reference material. I was also rather partial to the scoreboard I'd made in April out of aubergine sequins and six shirt cardboards for Skizzy Bickfield's Wingless Fly Races. Even then I knew these sorts of things and the *many* others like them were NOT Art. They were too much fun. Real artists—the ones I'd read about, anyway—lopped off their ears and starved themselves, twitching with demented fits in drafty attics of unredeemed squalor, only to be dragged in the dead of night to the Vatican and murdered by the pope.

Thank you, no.

But at the end of the day, you can't major in Making Stuff, so it was Art by default.

When I told Mom and Dad I wanted to be an Art major the floor practically came up to greet them. (Mom, near sobs: "Why didn't you tell us *before*? Maybe we could have *done* something . . . ") But they'd sooner see me convert to Catholicism than attend a trade school, so State it was.

Let me point out here, before you get the wrong impression: causing my mother and father any unearned stress or horror with this plan didn't even occur to me, and wasn't the point. I knew I was supposed to love my parents, and in fact, I was reasonably certain that I did; as one would fondly regard a reliable old sedan (with big soft seats) that started right up, even on frigid winter mornings, and practically never broke down. Or, better—two loyal, ageless farm cows, which besides everything else even let you ride them if you really wanted to. They could be counted on for an endless stream of milk, and should *that* ever be exhausted . . . well, meat. I should add that I gave them credit for about as much intelligence, a fact I now review with some regret.

As I do with most.

College? I was never too crazy about the idea in the first place, but not going didn't seem to be a choice—any more than not going through puberty. And it looked to be about a tenth as fun. Actually, it wasn't hatred of Art that led me to State at all, it was hatred of responsibility. In the face of this distant but charging train of education, I just ran along the tracks and alit onto the platform at the nearest station. Once decided, I put as little thought into it as possible. It was a necessary but potentially disfiguring operation, scheduled for the vague, impending future. At some point it would be over, so no sense in dwelling on it. What's for supper?

• • •

"That must be *it*." Mom's voice pulled the rug of sleep out from under me. "Dom, start moving over to the right lane, there'll be an exit soon." Then, noticing me, "You're *up*. Just in time. Want some juice?" She was already pouring. My mother was incapable of undertaking any car trip longer than twenty minutes without enough coolers, snacks, napkins, sandwiches, and cups to see us clear to Spokane without stopping. Livingstone took less when he explored the Congo.

Now she was referring to the complex of buildings that loomed in the valley below as we descended a mountain in the August noon heat.

"It's certainly big." She turned to my father. "And you made *such* good time, Dad. Were you speeding?" The idea—Dad speeding. Imagine Mercury loitering.

"No. Funny though, we shouldn't have gotten here this quick. Let's see the map, Took." Mom's nickname was Tookie. Did I mention that?

"Finish your hoagie first. What do you want to know? You should be in the right lane. Where's the stadium? I don't see the stadium. You're dripping."

"I don't think we're supposed to get off I-Eighty until after exit sixty-three. The last was forty-two. Is there anyone behind me? Can't see."

I looked out the right side window. "You're clear." We made our way over to the center lane. Even though I intended to bring only the necessities, somehow the rear of the station wagon was chockablock—clothes, books, blankets, pillows, desk and floor lamps, sweaters, thermos bottles, Dopp kit. My vast and stupendous Kukla, Fran & Ollie collection, which I methodically constructed over a six-and-a-half-year period and would always be tragically underappreciated by anyone but me, stayed at home—with the exception of my Kukla code-whistle nose siren (you never knew).

The university, from here, was even more imposing than I'd expected. Indeed, stately. My confirming letter from the Housing Authority said I was assigned to Mifflin Hall, room 613, and I tried to imagine its place among the structures now filling the landscape to the right. Nothing about a roommate was mentioned, which I took to mean I wasn't going to have one. This suited me just fine. I was already writing a request in my head to have my meals delivered to my room, so I could avoid the—

"DOM! It's this exit! You're not over far enough!" Mom's nerve-shattering wail shook the car. She clutched the dashboard for strength. At moments like these—they were not few—it occurred to me that if Job himself had married my mother, he would by now be a widower serving fifty-to-life.

"I TOLD you!!"

Or perhaps acquitted.

"We'll *miss* it!!"

A highway sign approached, and soared over head:

EXIT 43
STATE PENITENTIARY
CORRECTIONAL FACILITY
200 ft. KEEP RIGHT

Silence in the car. For a good ten minutes.

···

To give Mom a little credit, the real thing at a distance actually was a dead ringer for the State Pen, only *with* a stadium. There was a twenty-minute wait for the information hut at the entrance gate, and when we got there a stocky little guy who looked like the warden from *Stalag 17* gave us a map and barked that Mifflin Hall was at the north corner of the campus. It took another fifteen minutes to reach it as I studied the layout: Campus— *God*. It was a city, really.

No—a state.

My new home was a red brick affair trimmed with white granite and 1947 carved into its cornerstone. Someone had tried to train ivy up one side and had long since forgotten to water it. Eight floors, twenty rooms per, and one elevator. The four dorms faced in on a cement patch dotted with benches called The Quad, our own little Red Square. By my junior year, I would recognize this entire area as the realization of a freshman architecture student's rendering of Cost-Efficient Utopian Housing. *Before* he added the trees. He must have drawn people instead. Swarms.

Mom stayed with the Ford while Dad and I went to Mifflin Hall to get the room key, whereupon I got my first taste of State Hospitality—the associate housing proctor shuffled through a phone book's worth of documents before telling me I didn't have a room of my own after all. In fact, as it turned out I would be blessed with not just one roommate, but two: Vermont Foy, who was aptly named (rural, all right angles, sparsely populated, and often quite cold) and Thenson Helios (son of Greek immigrants; only one eyebrow, usually shaped like an inverted V in a state of perpetual apology). This was jarring enough, but the real fun began when we got to the room, built for—surprise!—two. All parties arrived within about ten minutes of each other and made uneasy introductions, sharing an irritated amazement at our circumstances.

Soon the resident assistant for our floor, Bob Burkenstock (prematurely balding, Class of '59, Hotel Management, shrill), showed up. He had us load most of our stuff in a storage closet at the end of the hall, put in a request for a cot, and assured us that our little Camp 613 would be thinned out in a couple of days, pending reassignment for one of us.

"Sorta thing happens all the time!" he said in his fire-alarm voice, as if living like a clump of newborn hamsters in a shoebox was a cherished State tradition. Christ, maybe it was.

• • •

"I just hate to leave you this way." They stood next to the car, nothing left to take out of it. Mom was referring to the room fiasco, but even if that had been square she still would have said it. Or at least thought it. She was a doll with the stuffing falling out, her button eyes hanging by threads. The dark half-moons under Dad's armpits somehow embarrassed me. Weren't these people ever going to leave? Emotional Scenes with underscoring and close-ups were strictly for the movies. This was agony. Why couldn't we have been English and sensibly frosty? I put my weight from foot to foot.

"I'll be fine, really." Please, please leave.

"They seem like nice boys."

"Yes." God, *please*.

"I'll miss you," she said with an unwarranted sadness, as if she was donating me to science against her will, and she gave me a small child's helpless hug and kiss. Dad shook my hand, vigorously—as if we were meeting for the first time and he wanted to make a good impression.

And then they were gone.

The back of the station wagon, *our* station wagon, was shrinking on the horizon, and everything changed. It was just impossible I was not in it. My heart started running for it and my legs almost followed. And like THAT, horribly, it wasn't as if I'd Escaped. I'd been Left Behind.

• • •

Eventually, roommates Vermont, Thenson, and I went to the dining hall together. Having originally thought we'd be dispersed quickly, we hadn't bothered to find out much about one another. But it had been going on a week now, with no reprieve in sight (Bob: "It's coming through! Keep hangin' in. You guys are the best. Really."), and Vermont finally asked what I was majoring in.

"Me? Art." Enough of that. "You?"

"No kidding?" Too late, the curtain was raised. Vermont looked as if I'd just told him I had smallpox. "As a career?" He probably wondered if I was contagious.

"Well, I just thought that I'd try it out." Then I offered, to ease his sudden concern: "I mean, I can always change it."

His manners kicked in. "No, I think it's great, that . . ." he groped for some positive angle ". . . someone actually *does* that." I knew what he meant—it was the way I felt about garbage collectors, veterinarians, and the military. He turned to Thenson and went on, grasping for humility: "I mean, I can't even draw a straight line, can you?"

Try a ruler and a pencil, you fathead. I changed the line of questioning. "Um, what are *you* majoring in, Thenson?"

"I'm undeclared." It wasn't an apology, just a state of affairs. "I thought I'd see how it goes for a while. I'm thinking about Accounting." Undeclared. Now why didn't *I* think of that?

"How long can you be undeclared?" asked Vermont, wary about this *status*, this academic atheism.

"End of sophomore year, if I want, but I'll figure it out before then." I was shamed—here was someone even more ambivalent about college than me. He asked Vermont, "What are you taking?"

"Well," he said, quite pleased, "I'm doubling in Ag Sci and Business. I'm going to take on my dad's golf course after graduation. Believe it or not, State is supposed to have the best turf management program in the country." He beamed, secure in the faith that training grass to look like carpeting was one of the Commandments. "Did you guys know that you can honest-to-God take golf here as a gym class? I mean, is that great or is that *great*?"

Soon the conversation shifted to the next day's main event, registering for classes. I thought it was just a formality, as we preregistered by mail in the summer. Vermont had asked around and didn't think so at all.

"Preregistration was so they could get a rough idea of who wanted to take what. Tomorrow is the real thing."

"Really? I didn't think it was that big a deal."

"Well," he balled up his napkin and lifted his tray, "the word is get there early. It's supposed to be a little nutty."

• • •

The university was divided into colleges; these were subdivided into schools, and the schools were made up of specific majors. Thus: Art was part of the School of Arts and Architecture, which was in the College of Liberal Arts. Registration times and places were different for each of the colleges. Mine was to start at nine in Burser's Hall.

I thought it rude to be early for anything, but I decided to take Vermont's advice and get there at five to. As I approached, I took in the group of people gathered in front, waiting for the doors to open.

There were, I'd say, just over a thousand of them.

A block away (as close as the crowd would allow) loomed Burser's—a monolith and something of an oddity on campus because, as one of the school's original buildings, it was actually old. At nine sharp its three pairs of doors parted and we began our influx into its depths. By nine twenty-five I ascended the steps. A second pair of doors opened and I went . . . onto the set of a DeMille-esque epic about Ellis Island at the turn of the century. But the director had fled because things were entirely out of hand. The din—an agitated, sonorous chorale—lit on every slick surface and recoiled, filling the cavernous room like a tank of warm, cloudy water.

A short, annoyed blond girl in an RA costume popped into view and bellowed an invisible question at me.

"What?!" I screamed.

"—taking? What's your MAJOR?!"

"Art?! ART!!" I sounded like Lassie. I made a frenzied scribbling motion with my hand. She looked at her clipboard and flipped a few pages.

"Line FOUR!!" she screeched, and pointed to the teeming horde.

"Where's THA—" Gone.

I was a lurching hobo of despair. The windows, our destinations, were numbered, and I tried to visually follow back from the queue at the fourth one, but in the middle of the room it shot off to the left around a structural pillar and fused into the throng. I headed to where it turned and started yelling its name—I was its frantic mother in a mobbed department store.

After five minutes of this I started imagining someone was answering me—a girl's voice with a southern lilt, and then I wasn't imagining it. A milk-white arm clutching a handkerchief rose a foot or so above the masses yards away and shook in my direction. "Over hee-yah!" I could just make it out, the words verbally embossed on the clamor. I navigated myself through the crowd and thought DeMille would have loved this scene had he stuck around to shoot it. I reached her and asked if she was the end of line four.

"This is it!" she chimed.

I took my place in back of her and pulled out my course catalog, to study for the long haul.

"I mean I hope so . . ." she added, less certain. I kept pretending to read and bobbed my head, eager to avoid a conversation. If we started talking now, we'd have to think up things to say for what looked to be hours.

"I'm pretty sure, at least." And she seemed equipped for that. She was chipping merrily away at the precious, fragile barrier that kept us Strangers. "Don't you think?" Small talk is small in every way except when you try to get around it. Then it's *enormous*. Defeated, I closed my catalog and really looked at her for the first time. She seemed completely out of place. Not just in this room, but perhaps in the entire state. She was dressed for, well, not for *this*, anyway. You don't wear ankle-length white linen at this hour to jockey for position in a viper pit. Nor for such an occasion does one "do" one's hair, though the only thing you could call her hair was Done. Her eyes gleamed bright with the fear that you Might Not Like Her, and her eyebrows met occasionally with the suspicion of the abandoned—maybe she thought she'd been left at the wrong school. She stood relatively still, but her spirit was dog paddling.

"I heard this was going to be out of hand," I offered, "but . . ." I let it trail off, and allowed the facts to finish it for me.

"Isn't it for the *birds*?" she asked, using a phrase my mother would say when there weren't any parking places at the Food Clown. "I mean *really*." Hers was the manner of someone who, as an impressionable youngster, saw *Gone With the Wind* a dozen times, scrutinized Vivien Leigh's every move and put a generous dab of Attar of Scarlett behind each ear.

But for naught: Her ample hips, underlying uncertainty, generous cheeks, and a forehead that launched a thousand anxieties all ran contrary to her aspirations. She was easily recognized for what she was and always would be—pure Melanie.

I was her captive in line for the duration and I learned a good deal about her, as one would from a misplaced child in a police station while awaiting the arrival of her parents. Her name was, cross my heart, Maybelle Lee. She was born outside of Augusta, Georgia, and moved up North when she was twelve (Daddy's company was *expanding*. She made it sound as if he owned it, which surely meant he did not). She'd always had that creative "itch," and she decided to scratch it by pursuing the Visual Arts, with the hope that someday she could "apply her acquired knowledge and amassed skill in a conventionally useful and lucrative way."

Exactly why I found her so irritating escaped me at first, but then I decided it must have been her sincerity—another trait that would bar her forever from O'Hara status.

Finally, it was Maybelle's turn to register. I listened with focused intensity while affecting a veneer of thorough ambivalence. After a short exchange that I couldn't make out, she turned to me with a start, her eyes frantic with desperation.

"We're—we're in the wrong place."

"What? Where—?"

"This is the Liberal Arts line."

Oh, for Christ's sake.

"I thought they were all for the College of Liberal Arts."

"Well, yes, but this is the line if you're *majoring* in Liberal Arts. I didn't know—"

Jesus. No no no. I motioned her aside and approached the window. I tried to assume the look of someone who is worthy of tremendous pity, yet also knows exactly where he is supposed to be.

"Ma'am?" The woman on the other side of the inch-thick sheet of glass (clouded with a greasy mosaic of hand and fingerprints) looked bright-eyed and eager to help, but also bore the scars of having heard it *all* when it came to these matters. This wasn't going to be easy.

"Yes, dear?"

"Hi. We're both Art majors and would like to register. We've been waiting an awfully long time . . . "

"Yes I know, honey, but this is the line for Liberal Arts majors *only*." She gazed benignly out at the surrounding hysteria and said, "I suppose the Arts line is one of the others."

"But we were instructed, specifically, to come *here*." This amused her.

"Oh, I don't think so, honey."

Undaunted, I went on. "But it's true. They said

you'd know all about it—that the Arts and Architecture and the Liberal Arts curriculums were remarkably similar, especially for freshmen. They said any line would do, actually." Then inspiration hit: "It's a new policy."

This switched a channel in her. Suspicious, conspiratorial, she leaned toward me and with a newly assumed gravity asked, slowly, "Did McGurk tell you that?"

I took on an air of confessional victimhood. I didn't have the slightest idea what she was talking about. "Well, yes, as a matter of fact, he—"

"That horse's HEINIE!" she yelped, then recovered her composure. "Sorry, dear, but he's been telling you kids all *sorts* of things this morning. He really ought to know better by now. Whillikers!" Her eyes narrowed then, just a bit. "Did he mention me by name?" The tag on her blouse read "Bert."

"Yes, I'm afraid so. He said, 'Bert in line four would understand. At least she *should*, by now ...'" I said regretfully, and slid my registration form through the slot. Bert heaved a great sigh and began to process the papers. I mopped my brow and turned to Maybelle—the thought of flight from this hellhole was making me giddy.

"What happened?"

"I think it's okay. I talked her into it. But if she yammers on about someone named McGurk, just roll your eyes and shrug your shoulders."

"Okay." She winked. There was a rap on the glass behind me. Bert was waving my form. Maybelle and I both went forward this time.

"The drawing class you wanted—Art 101—is filled at that time. In fact," she shuffled through sheaves of forms, "they all are, except for one—it meets on Mondays and Wednesdays, at nine."

"Okay—" Before I had a chance to add anything else, Maybelle bolted to life and mouthed through the glass:

"Yes! We'll *both* take it!!"

• • •

Later that afternoon, I walked through the gallery in the Visual Arts building. The day before, while strolling past, I saw something especially peculiar in it, but I was on my way to the Dean's office to pick up some forms and didn't have time to follow up. Now I went in and it was still there—in the middle of the room still showing last spring's Sophomore and Junior Sculpture exhibit. Amid the pint-sized mutant Rodins and accidentally abstract figure studies stood a large plaster column—or pedestal, rather. This would not have been strange had there been something resting on top of it. There wasn't. I thought at first they were still putting up the show or tearing it down, but no, neither was the case. I went in for a closer look and read the label at its base:

TITLE: 'Is NOTHING Sacred?'
          or, perhaps,
     'The Seventh Circle of the Cheese Monkeys'
MATERIALS: Large chalk garden ornament,
               Bagfuls of pretension,
               Hot air.
ARTIST: H. Dodd, '59., Vis. Ed.

It made me laugh. And not because it was stupid or awful. I thought: Bravo, Mr. Dodd, whoever you are . . .

• • •

ART 101. INTRODUCTION TO DRAWING.

INSTR.: DOROTHY SPANG, MFA
Mon & Wed., 9:00 a.m.
Room 210, Visual Arts Bldg.

DESCR: Using a variety of media (charcoal, conte crayon, pencils and the like) students explore translating onto the two-dimensional surface a range of traditional subject matter; including still life, the great masters, the human form, &c..

CREDITS: 3

On the first day of class, the Visual Arts building reclined before me like an old brick whore, egging me on to show her one, last, good time. I doubted I was up to the task, but regardless, I entered it from the rear, just to give myself the slightest mental edge. As I moved through the hallways, the works tacked to the corkboard lining the walls (mostly drawings on paper, from classes past and present) were at first very intimidating as a group—like the crowd at Yankee Stadium in game four of the World Series. But when you focused on them one at time you realized that divided they fell—all beer bellies and sweaty baseball caps.

Once inside, 210 looked like a high school stage set of an "art studio." The ceiling was two stories above us, an entire wall of windows allowed a generous light from the north, and everything smelled like petroleum. Nothing was clean or new. Several dozen paint-encrusted easels, each paired with a small worktable, were arranged in a semicircular arena around a central platform towards the front. I was trying to figure out whether or not we had assigned seats when someone grabbed my left arm.

"Well, here we are!" Maybelle was wearing a navy cotton shirtdress and a white cashmere sweater with mother-of-pearl buttons. She had brought enough art supplies to produce the Sistine ceiling. My relief at seeing her surprised me, but then it was probably due to what Uncle Joey referred to as the "Chinaman on the Moon" scenario. He coined the term when he was in the army, after a few too many transfers. "If you're in England," he'd say, "you're glad to see a Yank. If you're in China, you're happy to see a Brit. And if you're on the moon, you're happy to see a Chinaman!" In room 210 of the Visual Arts building, I was happy to see Maybelle.

"Think I brought enough?" Hmm—self-mockery or an earnest question? "If you need anything, let me know. I went a little crazy at Uncle Erbie's," which was the only art supply store in town. Outrageous prices. Erbie, an overgrown beatnik in his midforties, acted as if someone had just let him out of jail and he was getting even by charging two dollars for a piece of charcoal that wouldn't grill a guinea pig.

We took our places directly in front of the gray, coffin-sized pedestal, to get the best view.

At nine a woman came through the door with a giant Boscov's white sale bag in one hand and a mug of coffee in the other, announcing, "Hello everybody, just call me Dottie!"

Referring to a teacher by her first name was odd enough. A nickname seemed like nudity.

Were you to attend an opening for a Dorothy Spang show (with no previous knowledge of her or her work), you'd likely enter an otherwise empty room, notice her, and think, "Oh how sweet—at least the artist's mother showed up." Then you'd look at the drawings and change your mind to "Whoops! That *is* the artist . . . " She was the head of the Drawing Department, a mystery to the few who cared to ponder it. I imagined that her closest relatives felt she had great promise, urged her on like a gimpy racehorse, and had closets, TV rooms, breakfast nooks, basements, carports, and attics tiled with Spang originals. She was, as they say, Of a Certain Age, and favored dresses just below the knee made of fabrics left over from the pin-wale corduroy reupholstering of her living room sofa. Her scalp emitted a semicircular spoof of ivory hair—Bozo's grandma gone gray. Her nostrils were on a mad dash to either side of her face and her spectacles, bottle-thick lenses and frames of gilt-edged plastic, were perpetually refereeing the outcome. Behind them, her olive eyes shone brightly. They rarely pointed in the same direction, but at least they sparkled.

Dottie Spang didn't really *teach* Introduction to Drawing so much as she let it *happen* all around her. She also looked and behaved as if she just might know your parents.

The sole piece of information of any worth I retained from Dottie was something that I overheard her say in the middle of the semester to Rodney Hewitt, a particularly excitable member of the class who had just thrown his pastels out the window when it suddenly dawned on him that he wasn't Cézanne: "Remember, Robby," she said—her hearing wasn't the greatest—"no matter who you are, your first thousand drawings are always your worst." This was offered as encouragement.

Critiques for Dottie's class were every other Wednesday. We'd tack our papers up outside the room in the hallway, sit, stand, and slouch against the facing wall and were encouraged to speak up. Dottie's crits weren't exactly pointed—she liked everything. Or, at least, made the best of everything. I remember a drawing of a lion by Maybelle late in the term that looked as if she'd done it wearing a blindfold. Dottie soaked it in, slapped her hands together, tilted her head, and said,

"Oh, how brave! A placenta with a face! How did you ever think of that, dear? I never would have."

"But Dottie," I thought, "you just did."

For our first session, we started with still life. Dottie waddled up to the platform and set her burden on it with a thump. Then she removed from the paper sack an enormous wedge of Stilton cheese, a transparent medical model of a human kidney, a men's size 12 EEE cordovan wing-tipped shoe (no laces), a pomegranate, and a large stuffed, dusty, flightless bird (like a small flamingo or a kiwi, only blackish brown) missing its head. The creature was mounted, left leg in midstep, onto a pockmarked oval piece of peagreen wood that was pasted on the front with a bright red slab of label tape reading "RENALDO." A thick piece of coiled wire sprouted from its ropy neck—the scars of a taxodermic disaster long since passed. Dottie arranged these objects with the intensity of a chess champion.

"We want just the right amount of drama." Balancing the tip of the shoe on the pomegranate, she tilted it up towards Renaldo—whose adjustable neck she gently curved downward, so he and the footwear appeared to be having a conversation. The cheese stood demurely off to the left in the background, supporting the plastic kidney, which seemed poised to spring onto Renaldo's back and gallop away. Dottie stepped away from the scene and squeezed her eyelids together.

"It's just . . . not . . . enough." She rummaged through her bag and pulled out a crumpled velvet scarf the color of wilted dandelions and aswirl with Revolutionary War paraphernalia. She carefully draped a coat of arms over the kidney's edge, trained a Tory musket around Renaldo's left flank, and let a Minuteman march down past the shoe and over the side of the platform.

"There now . . ." she said, pleased. ". . . I think *this* is worth our attention." With that, she produced a thick, dog-eared paperback mystery, plopped herself in a chair, and started to read. It would be three classes before I got it: this was our cue to draw.

Maybelle was already hard at work, transferring the quixotic tableau onto paper. I reluctantly followed suit, wondering—wondering!—if Michelangelo started this way.

"I've never drawn an ostrich before," she said to me, "especially out of its natural environment. It's all so new, isn't it?"

"Spanking."

At the end of the class, Madame Spang roped off the display with tape and string, from which hung a sign that read "101 Still Life. Do not touch!"

I would have added "Or torch!"

• • •

My rooming situation, meanwhile, became less tolerable with each week, day, and minute. The first day's initial wave of despair, staved off since the move-in farce, began to seep back into the cellar of my well-being. And it was steadily rising, drowning delusions I only now awoke to—flimsy hopes that this would all be over in a few days and I could go back home.

No, not for four years.

Holding out for relief gave way to interior panic and tremors. Thankfully, Vermont started to rush the Ag Sci fraternity Alpha Gamma Rho (the Aggros), which kept him away till all hours, but it was always jarring when he'd finally stumble in, covered with grass stains, exhausted and reeking of fertilizer and cheap beer. Thenson, who must have left his personality in storage with everything else, studied in the room morning to morning, and when he wasn't doing that he was looking for me so he could latch on like a barnacle and ride me somewhere (to lunch, to the library, into town). I just longed for a place to be by *myself* . . .

During the second drawing class Dottie went to get a cloth to mop up after the hemorrhaging pomegranate, when my hungry eyes landed on a recessed loft, off to the upper back of the studio's rear. I stayed after the session until everyone had gone, and for a lark climbed the ladder leading up to it. Interesting: a mattress, a pillow, and group of thick votive candles. But it wasn't as if someone was using them, as far as I could tell—they were in storage—our next Dottie still life? Adventurous relief overtook me.

Officially, the Visual Arts Building was not open twenty-four hours a day, but I soon got wind from Rodney that the senior Painting and Sculpture majors made sure the back door was propped open with a brick after nine, for all-hours access. Regarding this, the Powers That Be at the school of A&A did what they usually did about everything (art especially)—looked the other way.

That first night I told myself I was just there to bone up on my sketching—the still life was intact, after all, and I was free to capture it as long as I liked. Back then I was still naive enough to believe that drawing a decapitated waterfowl would launch my career as a creative professional, and by God I'd do it till it ran flapping off the page.

But only fifteen minutes into my halfhearted scratching I gave up, and with the thrill of a novice-delinquent, I mounted the ladder and lit a match. An obscene, exhilarating idea: I could *sleep* here. The thought that Thenson might get worried sick if I didn't show up was a nag, but not enough to make me go back. I lit the candles, pulled out the mattress, and, sending dust everywhere, fluffed the pillow. I couldn't have felt more pioneering if I was on the Cumberland Trail. My sleep was fitful, afraid I'd be roused any minute with the order to Get the Hell Out. But no one bothered me. It was thrilling—so delinquent . . . so *La Bohème.*

• • •

After two weeks, 210 smelled like an over-worked professional wrestling team, the mummi-fied pomegranate had bravely given its all, and I had immortalized Renaldo the Headless Kiwi in graphite and one-hundred-percent cotton rag from every conceivable angle. He began to invade my dreams: My mother served him, stuffed and danc-ing, for Thanksgiving; we ran rhapsodically to meet each other across meadows set ablaze by the dying sun; and in a particularly gruesome episode, I gave birth to him at Hoskin's Hardware back home and nursed him for more than three hours. Ouch. Woke up to quite a mess—my undershirt was damp at the chest.

The third week of drawing class, we finally graduated to the human form. While kids were still shuffling in, a man in his late fifties or early six-ties—who couldn't have been more than five foot five—climbed onto the central platform in a ratty slate blue terry-cloth robe and crumbling orange flip-flops. Dottie placed a small gray block on the surface for him to put one foot up on. Had I seen this guy before?—But where? After everyone was seated, he threw off the robe to unveil at least two hundred pounds of flesh that looked like a pile of mud in a rainstorm. His hands were clumped into ham fists, and defiantly poked into either pillowy hip. As his head slanted upward, he gleamed with a puffy nobility—Lord of the Fluffernutters. He was, mercifully, not naked, but all that separated his privates from the public was a pair of boxer shorts that featured a pattern of pale yellow daisies. At least, in order to keep looking at them, that's what I made the shapes out to be.

The session was barely under way when a tiny voice—female—emerged somewhere behind me.

"Ahem."

I stiffened. How did a *nine-year-old* get in here? Maybelle returned my startled gaze.

"Miss Spang?" the voice inquired.

"Yes, dear?" Dottie awoke from her pulp reverie.

"I thought we were going to draw from the nude. That's what the course catalog said."

"Well, yes, dear," La Spang explained to the back of the room, "we had an undraped model on schedule to appear," adjusting her marshmallow tiara of hair, "but she took ill. So our own Mr. Peppie has graciously agreed to fill in at the last minute. Aren't we so lucky? Carry on!" She dove back into the depths of Agatha Christie.

A gas bubble of recognition rose from my bowels and popped in my head. Without his gray can-

vas jumpsuit Mr. Peppie's identity had been cam-
ouflaged, but I now remembered: he was the VA
building's custodian. I'd seen him day after day, lingering in the hallways at all hours with his mop and
bucket of disinfectant—eyes deep behind potato
sack lids, full of dull expectancies. Patiently waiting. For this?

Then: small clicking footsteps in back of, next
to, and on in front of me, continuing towards Mr.
Peppie. It was a girl in a lemon gunnysack, white
ankle socks, and tiny black patent leather pumps,
all under a dark bathing cap of hair. From the size
of her, she might have just come in from recess. She
motioned to the molten rock formation before her
to kneel, and he obliged. She whispered for half a
minute into his ear—his eyes to the left, to the
right, back again, then closed. He gave the shadow
of a nod, and stood with lopsided pride. Dottie
remained oblivious.

The girl launched herself on tiptoe, reached up
as far as she could, clasped the bottoms of the
shorts with each hand, and very, very slowly
pulled them down. The spent elastic waistband
sidled lazily over his hips and oozed down doughy
thighs like syrup on a stack of pancakes, before
dropping limply to the floor. Mr. Peppie stepped
almost daintily out of the cloth puddle and set his
right foot back on the block. The girl calmly folded
the boxers and placed them off to one side.

Maybelle looked up, released a small shriek, and

redirected her attention to the floor. Others did the same, united in horror. But I was mesmerized, as I had been in high school biology by projected slides of colossal African meat-eating beetles in midfeast. I confess I had never seen a foreskin before, and yes, I was not unaffected by its duffel bag of skin with the rope pulled tight, nestled under a tumbleweed of tired hair. But it was his scrotum which reminded me most poignantly of the sad fate of the flesh: the massive, sagging union of two rotten peaches, despairing in the Georgia sun.

Hello, Mr. Peppie.

The girl surveyed her handiwork. I half expected her to adjust the monstrous genitalia to her liking, but instead she pivoted, and stepped quickly back to her place. She paused briefly at my easel on the way, and took in what I had started to sketch. I returned the favor by scanning her face. I saw that she was indeed college age.

Her eyes: two black stars in a white sky.

But what really made my brain twinkle was her earrings. I later learned she made them herself, using plastic accessories from Lionel train sets—the miniatures used to populate the "towns" the toy engines sped through. Swinging from a thread-thin gold chain under her left ear lobe was the figure of a man, maybe an inch tall. He was clad in a dark business suit, his topcoat draped over his left arm, and his right hand was raised toward the hinge of her jaw. Had the technology of molding polymer been any more advanced, he would've held an anxious, long-ing expression stamped onto his BB pellet face. From her right ear hung a Lilliputian taxi cab, literally headed away from him. After a beat she was gone.

This was a girl I wanted to know.

About forty minutes later, I just couldn't stand it any longer and excused myself to go to the men's. On the way out, I located her easel, and creeping back in, snuck a look. Odd: she had cropped Mr. Peppie severely on the page, so all you saw was the the left half of his head from straight on and the top of his left shoulder. Her technique, I'd say, was better than average (no . . . excellent, actually)—neither styl-ized nor entirely representational—but there was no reason, based on her composition, for the subject to be nude from the waist down. Was it some sort of lark for her, to see if she could talk him into it? Or was she some fantastic new breed of reverse pervert, the likes of which had not yet been classified by the AMA? Certainly her drawing didn't depend on his nakedness one way or the other.

Back at my seat. Maybelle had recovered from the shock of Mr. Peppie in the altogether, and with the cavalier spirit of a Confederate captain interro-gating a Yankee prisoner, she proceeded with her drawing as if nothing had happened. When she got to his genitals (I just had to look), she imposed a seer-sucker fig leaf with the proportions of a lunch bag.

At the end of the session, Dottie got up to

address the class. It was too good to be true—from my perspective her head was just to the right of and level with Mr. Peppie's groin, an image that still keeps me warm at night: my own Comedy and Tragedy, carved over the proscenium of my imagination. I prayed like mad that the gods of righteous indecency would make her turn around, but by the end of her speech Mr. Peppie had relaxed and pulled his shorts back on.

Later, whenever I saw him in the hall, I was unable to shake the feeling that we shared a delicious, terrible secret.

• • •

In the middle of my fourth night spent in 210, I was awakened at two A.M. by giggles. At first I thought it was a dream, but there weren't any visuals. So I climbed down the ladder and cracked the door into the hallway's dimmed lights. It was the girl who had relieved Mr. Peppie of his skivvies. She sat, thin as a piece of tracing paper, on a hallway bench, facing the results of the life class. Her knees were pulled to her chin, her left hand clutching what was left of a fifth of Jack Daniel's. I only had the door open an inch or so—she couldn't see me. In her right hand was a sharpened piece of charcoal. Every couple of minutes she'd twitter like a child playing pin-the-tail, make her way to one of the drawings, and put something there. Then she'd replace herself on the bench, take another swig, and grin. This went on for another—what? half hour?—until she finally packed up and staggered away. Only then was I able to venture into the hall to see what she had been up to.

My eyes took a walk all over the wall, and didn't recognize anything amiss. Groggy, I was on my way back to the loft and to sleep when I took a last look at my own drawing.

It was fine. No, wait. Jesus.

Mr. Peppie had two left feet. In *my* drawing style. But I hadn't done that. And it now sported a title, in tiny lettering in the lower left-hand corner—"Vive la Danse." Son of a bitch. I went back over the others with a keener eye. Christ, they *all* had something wrong with them you'd never immediately notice. One sported two right thumbs, another's eyes were slightly crossed, yet another had a microscopic tattoo on his left thigh devoted to kitchenware, several of them had their crotches modified, with a realist's sober hand—all were altered in the manner of the original artists. The only one left untouched, of course, was hers. There it hung—with its odd cropping, just as it was on her easel.

"Gee," I thought. "I think *this* needs a little *something* . . ." I got my art supplies from the loft, returned to the girl's drawing, and went to work.

It didn't take long . . .

• • •

Later that day, during the critique for the Mr. Peppie Nude Class, I was certain everyone would recognize something was wrong. Not so. They all just sat there in the hall outside the studio, slack-jawed. Dottie was having a time getting anyone to speak up. I finally volunteered.

"I think it's great that people took a lot of chances." I looked the nutty girl in the eye. "I mean, like this." I pointed to my own drawing. "Two left feet, titled 'Vive la Danse.' Now, *that's* funny." The girl was not happy about this. She recrossed her legs and looked down the hall.

I advanced to Maybelle's drawing. "This is especially adventuresome, the heavy charcoal work under here." I pointed to Mr. Peppie's midsection. The Dixie fig leaf was gone. I ran my finger along the scrotum, now in lurid, full flower, "Bold. I think that's exceptional." Maybelle did her best not to betray her shock—manners and modesty kept her from spilling the beans. She nodded at the acknowledgment, but her face was clear: *"Thanks. That's enough. I don't know what's going on. Move along to someone else, please."* I did. To the wacky girl's. By now she was most distressed.

"This is great too." I circled her drawing with a vulture's grace. "The picture within the picture. I think that's very clever." She was pie-eyed.

"Really? What do you mean, dear?" asked Dottie.

"Well, in the center of the eye, very small," the girl was transfixed, "there's someone's face, the artist's I imagine." I was referring to the sketch I had put there not four hours ago, "Quite striking. I'd ask her about it . . . if I knew whose it was." Now I deliberately avoided looking at her. Dottie went up to the drawing to see what I was talking about.

"Oh, yes . . . isn't that something. Very like . . . Magritte!" She turned to address the class. "Whose is this?"

You could have parked a Buick in the space of the following pause. Finally,

"It's mine."

"Oh! What's your name, dear?"

"Himillsy . . ." she said, with a suspect's reluctance. "Himillsy Dodd." Him-*ill*-zee? H. Dodd—a girl?

"Well, dear. What a unique view you have. It's really very special."

"Actually," she replied, "I don't know what got into me," her eyes went hard into mine, "to do something so badly drawn. It really is a low point in my career here. I have a yeast infection. Please forgive me." She rushed to the wall, snatched her drawing, and made for the exit at the end of the corridor. I could see her though the doorway—she jammed the sheet into the stairwell's trash bin and tramped down the steps.

End of crit.

I gathered up my things and bolted, rescued the drawing from the metal cylinder, and continued after her. I caught up at a corner, waiting for the campus bus to pass. I stopped short of taking her arm.

"Hey!" I held up her drawing like a bagful of kittens she'd dropped in my river.

"Keep it, Caravaggio" she said without looking, and went to cross the street. I panicked.

"I mean, . . . I'm sorry!"

She stopped, turned, and lowered her sunglasses. Then she let my desperate stare ricochet off her face, and released this from her jelly mouth:

"We're *all* sorry."

And what does one say to that?

Not that I got a chance. She continued, as if picking up from a conversation we severed a month ago, "You know what has me really *steamed*, where you really screwed up?" walking towards me now.

"Where? Tell me."

She pulled the paper from my hand. Exhibit A. "I HATE Magritte! He ruined it for *everybody*— he gives anyone with an accelerated imagination a bad name! A face in the eye. *Really*. It doesn't look anything like me. It . . . it looks like Betty-God-damned-Boop! I would never have done that! I'm *beyond* it. It's such a *cliché*."

Who the *hell* was McGreet?

"Oh. Sor . . ." I checked myself. "Where are you off to?"

"The Diner." The entitled victim: "Buy me lunch."

I had a geo-sci class in ten minutes that I really couldn't afford to miss. I said, "Okay."

● ● ●

"I'll have a Linebacker burger with pickles, mustard, ketchup, lettuce, mayo, and french fries. And a large black cow Rah-Rah. Thick." She handed the unopened menu back to the waiter. "Then coffee and a Touch-Down sticky bun—toasted, extra goo."

"I'll have a regular hamburger and a lemon Coke." I had to be careful. Off-campus food expenses weren't exactly in my budget.

She took a cigarette from her pack of Camels, tamped one end of it onto the Formica tabletop three times, and licked the hollowed paper. Then she produced a Zippo lighter nearly the size of her hand, fired it up in a single expert gesture, drew in the smoke, and seemed to forget about it as it leaked slowly out of her nose and mouth. Someone else might have said she had a child's body, but *she* wouldn't, so you quickly changed your mind. Her elfin fragility from across the room became unbreakable Bakelite up close. Ray-Bans were perched atop her head above one of those silent movie faces that could say just about anything without a peep. She was wearing a man's pink Oxford shirt with the initials GMG monogrammed in black about four inches below her left breast. She swam in it. Her legs were in black pedal pushers, and her cat's feet, in avocado ballet shoes, dangled just above the floor. No earrings today, only posts. She was looking off to the distance behind me, and didn't seem to be in a mood to talk. I hated situations like this, however rarely I was in them—usually people around here were dying to tell you everything.

"I . . . I liked your column sculpture a lot," I started weakly, trying to flatter her by acknowledging her "career," "I mean, 'Is NOTHING sacred?'—that was yours, wasn't it?" Still not looking at me, she nodded once. "It was a riot, really, but I was wondering—"

"Do you know much about science?" she interrupted, finally releasing the smoke to the side of the booth.

"A little."

"Well," she tapped an ash into the foil tray, "what's the *story* with these balloon people?"

I waited for her to continue. In vain. "Um, I don't know what you're—"

"I can see wanting to go around the world in a balloon. That I can see. It's lunatic, it's something to *do*, and the whole rest of it, but they're overlooking the obvious. No?" Left eyebrow arched, she took another drag and held it in.

"Could you—"

"Don't you read *The Collegian*? I mean, I know it's a fishwrap, but what else is there?"

The school newspaper—yes, I read it first thing

every morning, though for obvious reasons, didn't get a chance today. And now I made the connection—it was being reported daily—a group of graduate students in the Meteorological Department were making noise about attempting to circle the globe in a hot-air balloon for the first time. Hugely pointless.

"Overlooking what?"

"That's what I wanted to ask you. You look square enough to know about this kind of thing," she leaned forward, to see if I was insulted (hardly—she was so *pretty*), saw I wasn't, and suddenly we were old friends. "Now, stop me if I'm insane, because I'm not a goddamned science major, Christ knows, but," very excited, "instead of having the balloon go around the world, why don't they just do the opposite?"

The opposite?

"Look, the Earth *turns*," she went on, "why go anywhere? You send up the balloon, okay, in ONE spot. Alright?—*Keep* it there, and let the whole sonuvabitch world pass under it in twenty-four hours! End of trip! Is that so hard?"

Whoa. "Wind currents." I parried, partially making it up. "It's a balloon, not a helicopter. It can't stabilize its position. It can't stay in one place." Her face fell.

"Shit."

I feared she was taking it personally.

"Sorry."

"Oh well, so much for that." She put her cigarette out of its misery.

The food arrived.

"Pardon me for asking," I tried to be the soul of discretion "but, do you really have a . . ." I didn't really want to say it. She looked at me sideways.

"*What*."

"A. Yeast, problem."

"What? Jesus, no. I needed an exit line. No one ever questions it—what are they going to do, prop up my skirt and dig around?" She picked up the burger. More than half her head disappeared behind it.

The sandwich was gone in under two minutes. She made short work of the milkshake too.

"What," I started, once the plates were cleared, "what do you think of Dottie?"

"What . . ." she lit up again, "do I *think* . . .?" She didn't bother to finish the question. Obviously she didn't think of Dottie at all. "I think," she sent a cloud of smoke to the ceiling fan, "that she couldn't teach a piece of shit how to stink." Another drag. "I also think she gets her decorating tips from Ripley's Believe-It-Or-Not, and . . . if I don't squeeze an A out of that lousy meatbag, I can kiss what's left of my grade point average good-bye, so Daddy can finally yank me out of here like a festering tooth."

"An A? For talking an octogenarian out of his underpants?"

"*That* was an aesthetic decision."

"Aesthetic?! Whose? Boris Karloff's?"

"Please. And he's only fifty-*nine,* for Chrissakes."

"But you drew his *head. Half* of his head."

"Exactly. Think about it."

"What did you say to him, anyway?"

"Don't change the subject."

"Okay." I leaned back, thinking out loud. "You were going to draw half his head. So naturally he needed to air out his what's-it to get the desired effect."

"Yes." Aiming her face at me. "Now, why?"

I hated to admit it—I was stumped.

She sighed. "If you were shoved up in front of the class in your bvds, you'd have a certain look in your eye—maybe interesting, maybe not. Take your undies away and it would, *at least*, be more interesting. No?"

Aha. "Alright, maybe. But drawing on everyone else's? You can't just do that. It's . . . sacrilege." And you didn't exactly appreciate it yourself, dear.

"No. Clogging the hallways with pukey drawings—*that's* sacrilege." She leaned in again. "Look. I was unable *not* to. Hey—you're driving down the highway. Someone runs up towards your car screaming 'Help me!,' what are you going to do? You stop. You help."

"Or speed up . . . "

She laughed—her thoughts exactly. "It was a

kick. And it's not as if I ran amok through the Prado with a hacksaw, or that those talentless clods in 101 would be any the wiser. People never notice anything." She took another drag. "What tipped *you* off?"

"You kidding? '*Vive la Danse*'?"

"Oh, I know. Isn't it terrible? I never know when to *stop*. I would have put new arms on the Venus de Milo."

"And nail polish, and bracelets, and elbow guards . . ."

"And sparkly breast pasties and rouge!" She was delighted. "And a fox stole, with a little freeze-dried head, and toothpick legs!" She leaned back. "Oh, why can't the world be *interesting*?"

The waiter brought her coffee and sticky bun, which leaked steam and looked like a wet gerbil hugging its knees. She let four pats of butter slowly die on it before insinuating her fork.

"But seriously," she said between mouthfuls, "*there's* a good example—about alteration."

"What."

"The Venus de Milo. Do you really think anyone would give a good whoop about it if it was intact? Okay, maybe it would still be stuffed away in some museum, but we wouldn't know about it, I wouldn't be talking about it right now. It—*she's* in our heads because she has *personality*." She sipped her coffee, her eyes darting from side to side. "What she's missing intensifies the effect of what she's got. It's a symbol . . ." She was figuring something out. Her face darkened. "She's a woman as men want her: a nice set of knockers and no fists or fingernails to defend them. You're all *pigs*."

"Now, wait a min——"

"You . . . you just want her at your mercy."

"And *you* just want to put tassels on her . . . you know. That wasn't *my* idea."

"*That* was in the spirit of fun!" She eased up and smiled. "I just want her to *live* a little, poor thing. Stuck in the Louvre all day."

The loove? "If it's any consolation," I offered, "she's got it made, next to Renaldo the headless kiwi." This tickled her. She picked up her mug of coffee with her pinky extended and spoke in the manner of a catty English lady at tea.

"Is *that* his name? I've often wondered across a crowded room. I suppose his features *are* rather Latin—*bathed* in mystery. We *must* put him on all the lists!"

"Haven't you *heard*?" I responded, doing my Laurence Olivier and not missing a beat, "he's spoken for. Engaged to Miss Wingtip. The romance with the Stilton girl crumbled and soured. Lady Spang is just *destroyed*."

Howls of laughter. Then she took a last gulp and said, "Come on. Let's blow this dump. Let's head to the Skeller."

Egads.

"It's three in the afternoon. It's Wednesday." I

had Art History at four. I just didn't do things like this. I was too young.

"Good. We can still get nickel jars."

• • •

I couldn't picture Himillsy Dodd at the Rathskeller anymore than I could see her candy striping in a leper colony. Its reputation was scalding. If State were on the water, the Skeller would have been a greasy drain under a rotten pier at the end of the wharf. Townies only—students entered at their own risk. A common fraternity hazing ritual sent pimply pledges into the place clad in nothing but pink and green, with orders to stay until closing. Few emerged intact. For me it was still a legend.

"Hey, Joey," she said to the hulk propping up the doorjamb, throwing her head my way, "he's okay. No sweat." We slid past his slow eyes and descended steps into the greasy murk. My Art History slide lecture was nicknamed Darkness at Noon, but it had nothing on this place. Something crunched under our feet—it could have been peanut shells, but it also could have been bacteria the size of poker chips. A wet film coated the stone walls and returned through a haze the dim glow of four no-watt bulbs dangling from long cords.

Everywhere smoke, smoke, smoke.

Several shadowy patrons in plaid flannel and worn denim lurked along the edges of the bar. They ignored us and went about the business of forgetting yesterday, today, and tomorrow.

I won't go into the smell.

We sat across an oaken slab chewed crazy with knife marks. I was afraid to touch anything, so I set my elbows on the table and kept my hands in the air, like a surgeon waiting for rubber gloves.

A tall, thick, bullet-headed man with a dark hole where his left ear used to be sauntered up to us, pointed his face at Himillsy, and said, "Hello, little missy." I was about to seize her by the wrist and run for our lives when I recognized the phrase—it was the way Punjab referred to Little Orphan Annie.

"Hey, Greck." She was cool as a cuke. Took out a fresh pack of PMs. "What's the temp?"

"High in the sixties, baby."

"I hear ya. Two slurp 'n' burps."

"You baby-sittin' or what?" He was looking at her but nodding at me.

"He's alright. He's on safari."

Greck pulled his mouth into a smile. "Spark?"

"Swell."

He took the match from his teeth, struck it against his left temple, and offered it to her: Me Greck—girl take gift of fire.

She leaned into it. "Thanks, G." He went to the bar.

I started to breathe again. "I can't believe I'm sitting here."

She broke her icy facade, bubbling. "Isn't this place the *end*? God, I love it!" Then a pause. "I never bring anyone here." Startled, eyes pleading and suspicious, as if this wasn't her idea in the first place. "Why did I take you here?" Stumped by her own question. We sat. Finally I broke the silence.

"Because tomorrow *someone* has to explain what happened to the police." This did not amuse. I fumbled. "Say—tell the bulldozer that if he doesn't hurt us, I'll make a new ear for him out of salt dough."

She gave her ash a flick. "Don't be *mean*. Greck adores me. He's a *lamb*."

"No, he's a side of beef. With a Van Gogh complex."

She betrayed a smile. "Oh, dry up." Thank God—she was shifting into second, then third gear. Fourth couldn't be far away. "Tell me it's not a relief to be in the only place within twenty miles where someone isn't waving pom-poms in your face."

"True." I squinted at her. "A slurp 'n' burp?"

"My little name for the house special—a boilermaker. Trust me."

Greck brought the drinks—two pint mason jars of rusty liquid. Each held a submerged shotglass filled with something dark brown—I wouldn't have poured it down a drain for fear of ruining the pipes. Himillsy gave hers a hoist and pointed it in my direction. "Down the hatch, natch!" She snorted and took a mouthful big enough to float a goldfish.

"Right." I lifted my jar. I probably don't have to tell you that I was not a drinker. Not then.

But I had to try it—I didn't want to be impolite. I jerked back my head, braced myself, and took a gulp. A malted cotton glove of beer slipped onto my tongue. Within seconds it had become a soda on fire, laying a trail of gasoline down the asphalt of my throat. The whiskey's match ignited it. The pain flared and thrilled. I tried to talk through the wall of flame, but it came out a whisper.

"Nice," I managed.

"It gives me such perspective. Don't things seem more clear to you already?"

"Somewhat."

"See!" The blinds were lifted between us. "So . . . you and that Dixie chicken seem to be pretty tight."

"What, Maybelle?" I sputtered, "We're just friends. Not even that, really. I met her at registration and we both ended up taking Dottie's class. She's nice enough. Little windy, though."

"She's a birthday cake with legs." Himillsy made her left eye a slit. "May bell?"

"Maybelle Lee."

"No."

"Yes. Right hand to God."

"What a riot." Threw back another swallow.

"So," I said, between coughs, "are you a Sculpture major?" This put a wry smile on her face.

"Was." A small belch. "Pardon. Or as I called it:

'Go Shit Nicely in the Corner,' which was all they ever want you to do. And before that, Painting, or: 'Pounding the Pigment.' Preceded by Textiles. And at the beginning, Ceramics—AKA 'Hi! My Name Is Mud!' "

"And, have you—"

"Been thrown out of each? Yes. I am—" she paused for effect, "Joan of Art."

"Oh. Need a match?" I quipped. "Actually, you should tell Dottie that you keep hearing voices telling you to lead the class to rise up and drive all the English majors out of the building. You should come to class in armor. On horseback. We should get Dottie into our confidence and then convince her that Maybelle is a heretic." Where was all this coming from? "In league with Renaldo. See if she has any suggestions. Keep her guessing." By now she was practically choking. She later confessed to me that I was the only person, besides herself, who could make her really laugh. It was the best grade I ever got. "C'mon, really, Mr. Peppie—what did you say to him?"

She wiped her mouth and cleared her throat. "I told him I wasn't good enough to draw it from memory." I nearly coughed up my drink.

Then out of nowhere she became serious and peevish. Not at me, but at an enemy we were united against. "I've just *had* it with this faux-primitivism in the arts. 'Abstract' daubs. Symbolic, bleak little plays. Junk sculpture, nihilistic, 'avant-garde' robotic verse. Crude banalities. Is that what we need?" Shrieking. "Is that what feeds the human heart? Is the human heart ABSTRACT?!"

No one looked at us. Sudden, freakish outbursts seemed welcome here.

"No. Not mine, anyway." Not that I knew what she was talking about.

My longing for someone fun to talk to made Himillsy the lightning bug in my honey jar. I punched holes in the lid so she could breathe. "The subtitle of your sculpture—who *are* the Cheese Monkeys?"

And then the roles traded places.

She snickered through her nose, crossed her eyes, and did a frighteningly accurate imitation of my voice. "So, just who *are* these cheese monkeys? And what do they *want*?" She gave herself to giggles. I knew better than to ask again.

"Actually," she straightened out, "that's sacred— strictly off limits. But I'll give you a hint, as a trade."

"For what?"

"An explanation."

Uh-oh. That's what I was afraid of. Whether she realized it or not, *this* was why she'd brought me here.

"I gave the class *oeuvre* a face-lift at about three this morning. VA doesn't open till eight-thirty, class started at nine, and crit at ten-thirty." She sipped, "So when the hell did you get a chance to wave your magic wand without anyone seeing?"

I considered this carefully. "Can you keep a secret?"

"Mmmm."

"Good. So can I."

Fierce stare. "Bastard."

"Sorry." As if it weren't up to me. I took another furry swallow. Her glass was nearly empty, and she sent her peepers on a trip around the room in search of Greck, found him, and nodded. Billie Holiday's buttermilk voice poured in from somewhere: "Good Morning, Heartache." Himillsy shut her eyes against the raptures. "God. Anyone who doesn't dig the Lady is just down here on a *visit* . . ."

"Without a map," I said, empowered by drink. Greck brought two fresh jars, though I still had a good third of my first to get through. I drained more of it.

Soon I no longer cared how filthy everything was, and the most pleasant sensation descended— not just the booze, but . . . it was the first time in two weeks I didn't feel homesick. My mind was putty on a Sunday funnies page, pulling up images and twisting them to my liking. I yanked Greck's sides outward, leaving him a squished, helpless dwarf. I gently coaxed Himillsy taller and let down her hair. I made her eyes a little softer. A little happier.

"What're you staring at?"

"Sorry, I. So what, now, for you, then?"

"What."

"I mean, what's your next major? You should've had Intro to Drawing a long time ago."

"Put it off. Kept waiting for something really awful to happen to dotty Dottie." She affected remorse. "No luck. I'll probably end up a Liberal Arts nun. Garnett says I won't know what I want to do till I leave here anyway. Till I'm free of the *tyrannie de l'Académie*. It's one of the few things we agree on."

Garnett. The way she said his name, as if he was a given, something she was born with—Garnett was not just some friend. Of *course* Himillsy was going steady. People who looked like Himillsy were always going steady, the way people who looked like me always carried something to read. So why did this disappoint me so? The initials on the shirt—his? I wanted to know everything about him, about *anyone* who might hold her interest. Without trying to sound too nosy, I asked, "What's his calling?"

She screwed up her eyes again and spat out, "Architecture. He's learning how to take God's green earth and square it off. Man's Inhumanities. For credit."

"That must be very—"

"Geometric. Concrete. Self-important. Reason-based. A snore."

"But Jeez, we gotta have them. I mean . . . there was some architect that built this place, right?"

"No, there wasn't. That's my point. Whoever built this place wanted to keep the rain off a bunch of juice pigs long enough so their dough wouldn't get soggy before he could poison them and grab it.

Period. It's honest. Mies van der Rohe couldn't design a dive—or any other place for *human beings*—if his crispy life depended on it."

"Who?"

"Skip it."

We talked about something else after that, though I couldn't say what, and I think I had at least half of my second drink. Then we were at her car, a smart little white Corvair two-seater, and she must have asked if she could drop me somewhere. I guess I said yes. It was dark and I remember I thought it was very late, but then realized it wasn't at all. She opened the door to let me in and it was just amazing because it was one gigantic ashtray inside—every inch of the floor and dashboard held fistfulls of ashes and butts and gum and candy wrappers and spent matches. She giggled and started the engine. Then we were headed back towards campus, doing sixty at least. I was not feeling well. Sweating—in October. I needed a tissue. I fiddled with the glove compartment.

"Hey. Hands off. Don't—" The door popped out. I saw it. Oh.

Oh. Oh. My God. Horrible . . .

"I warned you . . ." she said, with mild disapproval.

"Oh. Dear Heav—." I shut it. That was it. All I needed. I started to heave and wretch. Himillsy stayed calm and issued orders.

"You can't shlarf in my car. Really. I'm serious."

She rounded a corner. We were in the middle of Main Street, people everywhere. No place to stop. "There *are* limits. Roll down the window." I fumbled for the crank. "Do it. Now! I mean it!" I was a puppet with the strings cut. Unnameable forces guided my hand to the knob and made orbits. The window descended and my head went over. The tragedy in my stomach raced up my gullet and burst out of my mouth—Act I, Act II, Act III. The acid taste scraped over my tongue before it exploded onto the public sector, streaming down the side of the car. Someplace in my powerless mind I worried it might take the paint off the chassis. Suddenly it became imperative to me that we keep moving— forever. Pedestrians, curious, then appalled, sped by to the right. I returned my thoughts to the horror in the glove compartment and offered more out into space—there seemed to be an endless supply. We stopped at a light. Himillsy was in hysterics, waving at everyone and shrieking. "Hi Biff! Hi Midge! It's so great to see you! Spewy says hi!" She gave me a nudge. "Spewy, doesn't Midge look fabulous?"

"SHLAAAARRGGAAHH! GRRAAAAG!"

"Oh, Spew! You never did go in for PLAID! Sorry Midge! 'Bye kids!!" It changed to green and we were off.

I spent the rest of the night in a Mifflin Hall lav (two floors below mine, for discretion's sake), making deposits into the porcelain every hour or so, until all I could do was wretch tortured breath. I promised God I'd never drink again if He'd just let me stop heaving, but He didn't get my call until late the next morning.

• • •

ART 101. INTRODUCTION TO DRAWING.

(cont'd)

Wherein we measure the merits of gestural studies.

Over the next day and a half I slowly, slowly returned to the world. The singing pain in my head was backed by a chorus of terrible guilt—a sense that the entire school's reputation had been irrevocably marred by what I had done. When I was able to go out, I couldn't help but feel everyone I passed knew I'd yawned in Technicolor all over Main Street. I missed half my classes and told Thenson I came down with stomach flu. I decided I would keep my promise to God and never touch a slurp 'n' burp again—not the hardest declaration to make. How Himillsy could put away two jars of that hemlock and stay as sober as a straight line was something I was going to have to ask her at Dottie's next class. If I had the nerve.

I was on the cusp of whether to be furious with her or apologetic in the extreme (God, her *car*!).

And then of course, there was that matter of the—jeez, it hurt just to think of it—the *thing* in her glove compartment. Surely I imagined it. Demon rum.

• • •

"You look a little under the weather." Maybelle adjusted her easel. "If I do say. Are you ill?"

"Um, I'm getting over a little stomach flu. I think the worst of it's behind me. But it's been a rough couple of—"

"Oh! That's just too *awful*. My Uncle Langdon (Lanky, we used to call him—*such* a great dancer) once ate a tired oyster at a low bar in Charleston and didn't see the outside of his commode for almost a week—"

"Is this seat taken?"

Himillsy: in a little boy's navy sailor suit, complete with white cotton canvas cap, brass buttons, and a khaki knapsack. I thought I was hallucinating.

"Hi!" I was already pulling the stool next to me out for her. I introduced her to Maybelle.

"Charmed. That's such an interesting name." Mabes tried to pronounce it.

Himillsy corrected her. "Accent on the *ill*, dear. Yes. It's Lithuanian for 'Tiny, Ugly Failure.' Mums and Dad were quite the prophets." She went about unpacking her art supplies.

Maybelle couldn't decide if she was serious or not. It wouldn't be the last time. "Oh, that's—"

Dottie swooped in, carrying a canvas bag and a good-sized cardboard box poked with holes.

"Hello, everybody! Today we're going to do Gesture Drawings. Do you know what that is?"

Hims eyed her with suspicion.

"Gesture drawings are very quick studies, an exercise to keep your minds and fingers nimble. Very immediate. Visceral. Not labored." While she was saying this, Dottie removed a leash made of chrome chain and a glass pitcher from the bag. She affixed the handle end of the chain to a rail spike driven into the center of the wooden platform where Mr. Peppie had stood only a week ago. Then she opened the lid on the box and removed an enormous tortoiseshell cat. She hoisted him chest level.

"Everyone, this is Colonel Percy Boomer. He's just a little kitten. Say hello, PB." She rapidly wagged his right paw up and down. Percy looked a little, well, *used*, shall we say. And he was thirty pounds if he was an ounce—his kitten days were a bygone era. He seemed exhausted by life, and his left eye couldn't open all the way. "He's our subject today." To his weary indifference, she kissed the top of his head, then set him down and attached the leash to his collar. He couldn't go more than a yard or so in any direction. She picked up the pitcher and trotted into the hallway.

"It won't be uninteresting." Himillsy's tone was grave. "I've heard about this, but I never believed it."

"What?"

Colonel Percy, tethered, was pacing groggily, in a kind of fearful anticipation. Dottie returned, hoisting the pitcher—filled with tap water. She put it down and donned an old smock.

"Okay. Gesture drawings, as their name suggests, must be done with great speed. You have to try and capture the moment—let your fingers do the thinking. Get out your black conte crayons, everyone. Are you ready? Focus on Colonel Percy. He is poised at the ready. Colonel, may I?" She picked up the pitcher.

No. She wouldn't.

"Here we go!"

With that, she raised it and turned it over onto the cat. Percy made a noise like a baby being boiled alive and bolted in five directions at once. I wanted to cover my ears, but I was too busy scribbling. The miserable animal flailed, jerked, and shrieked. Pins of water shot everywhere and dribbled down the sides of the platform.

"Are you all getting that? Don't be frightened. He's having the time of his life! Fill a page and then rip it away. Not more than ten seconds on each one. Nothing's precious! Discipline yourself!"

Maybelle was at first frozen by the spectacle, but soon thawed and got down to business.

Himillsy: fascinated.

"Oh my God, it's brilliant." Her hand was dancing over the page. "Dottie's *insane*. The chain will snap and Percy Boomer will kill us all. His vengeance will be swift and terrible. Many will die—look at him."

I did. We all did. It wasn't easy. Everyone worked like mad.

Dottie trotted out to fetch another pitcher of water.

At break, Maybelle got up to stretch and went to the ladies'. Colonel Boomer lay breathing heavily in a sopping heap, probably working out the details of his merciless war on mankind. Hims and I were as alone as we were liable to get. She sat and studied her work—a furious cacophony of lines which mapped out a vision of the mental state of the animal in a truly disquieting way. And, I suspected, a little too insightful. So much better than mine, which looked like discarded storyboards from a Tom and Jerry cartoon.

"Um, I'm sorry about the other night. I mean, your car . . ."

"No sweat. It needed a new paint job anyway," she glanced over and grinned, "Spewy."

"Oh, God. Listen, I have to tell you. I've never been drunk before—"

"Really."

"I mean, I only remember . . . less than half of it. But I wanted to ask you . . . "

"Yes?"

"When I, opened the glove compartment, in your car, by mistake, I thought that—"

"You saw this." She leaned down and opened her knapsack. There it was. Yeek.

"Oh. Oh." The familiar nausea was awakening. She zipped it up again. In pain, I asked "W-What *is*—?"

"Later," she whispered sharply, nodding to someone behind me.

"How's our little Colonel Boomer?" Maybelle walked up to the platform and put her hand out towards the furious pile of sodden fur. Percy looked at her and issued a low, weighty growl.

"Um, I'd back off there, Maybelle," I said.

"He's a furry ball of cold, soggy hate, dear," chimed Himillsy, in a perfect Dottie voice. "Unless you'd like to wake up in intensive care trying to remember your name, you'd best retreat."

"I suppose you're right." She reluctantly backed away. "Poor thing . . . "

"Oh, he's having the time of his *life*," Hims went on, "why, by tonight he'll be wearing his special *wig* and dancing over red coals while we poke him with *sticks*—he's such a *card*! All he ever cared about was our *happiness*. So *giving*, the darling."

Dottie returned with a fresh pitcher and we went back to work.

I soon found there's nothing quite like a knapsack at your feet with a dead baby in it to cramp your drawing style; to say nothing of trying to put pleasing marks on paper with the suspicion that the person next to you is really a fiendish ghoul in the guise of the illegitimate offspring of Popeye and Betty Boop. Add Percy's infantine screams and I had the makings of forty-five minutes that seemed to go on for weeks.

When class was finally over, I very cautiously trailed Himillsy outside.

"That was too much," she said, waiting for me to catch up. "Maybe Dottie's got a trick or two left. Let's go to the Creamery. Today's caramel."

"I . . . have to get to Art History."

"It'll *wait*." She was on her way, her pull irresistible, tidal. "It's not like it's *going* anywhere . . ."

• • •

Dairy farming was practically a religion at State and Ice Cream the sacrament. Only two blocks away from the VA building, the Creamery provided an altar for all those shuddering udders. Milk products I didn't even know existed lined its refrigerated cases (cheese curds, anyone?—only a dime a bag!) but it was the twenty-cent cones that had kids lined up out the door—even in January. A sign over the counter boasted "only four days from cow to cone!" Lucky for us it was before the lunch rush and practically empty. Hims ordered two scoops of caramel and I got one of vanilla. We planted ourselves at one of the tables along the edge and lapped away. Hims started to giggle.

"What," I asked. Her gurgling intensified. "*What?*" She settled down, but her voice was a singsong.

"You should have *seen* everyone on the side-walk—they were just *mortified*! It was fabulous." She tittered some more.

"Jeez. Thanks a lot."

Finally, I just had to: "Himillsy. Um, what *is* . . ." I looked at her knapsack. She thought a moment, then set her cone in one of the holders mounted on the table. She checked to see if anyone was paying attention. Satisfied, she unzipped.

"This," she lifted it out, "is Baby Laveen. He's a Republican, but I love him."

I was flooded with relief. It was a doll—a breathtakingly realistic replica of an infant, made out of soft, flesh-toned rubber. Baby Laveen was frozen in that stage (what—one?, two weeks?) when babies don't look quite as horrifying as they do in the very beginning, but still have at least a month to go before being adorable. I had only seen his head in the glove compartment and assumed that Himillsy had . . . well, no point in thinking about it now.

He was dressed in a man's gray flannel suit—superbly tailored to his body—with a tiny white oxford broadcloth shirt accented by a maroon tie, knotted in an impish four-in-hand. A campaign button on his minuscule left lapel beamed "I like IKE!" He looked like a postfetal board member of

Babies Corp. Beguiling black leather wing tips the size of matchbox cars housed his feet. She wagged his right arm like Dottie and the Colonel. An eerie image—the parent and the child had switched clothes.

"Daddy's a big fat pediatrician. Teaches at Yale." She set Baby Laveen on her knee. "When I was three, my baby brother, DeVigny, was born. He was named for the French poet." She became quite serious. "I adored him." She adjusted the doll's collar with expert care. "He died, very soon after. Infantile paralysis. I was inconsolable." Hims looked out the window. "They make these replicas to use in the classroom. For professional instruction. Daddy gave me him to play with and take my mind off things. I called him Laveen—I never could pronounce his name right. He's been my best buddy ever since." She turned him to face her. "Haven't you?" she asked him soberly, as if she wanted to borrow a quarter.

A million questions were born in my mind: Why would a responsible father—a presumably respected child care specialist, no less—provide and foster this sort of artificial and flimsy emotional compensation for his daughter? And why hadn't she outgrown it? What was Mr. Garnett, the Architect's take on BL— if he even knew about him? Was I supposed to find it amusing?

I did, by the way. He broke me up. I guess that answered that.

"Pleased to meet you, Mr. Laveen." I tugged his clammy little hand. Ha ha. I got up. "I have to get going. To class."

"See you Wednesday?" she asked, picking up her cone. I looked for a little hope in her eyes and found it—just barely.

"Of course." Then I added, touched that she'd care, "It's not like I'm *going* anywhere . . ."

The three of us—Hims, Maybelle, and I—formed something of a de facto alliance in Dottie's class during the next few weeks, though it existed strictly inside the classroom. Once the session was over, Hims would skitter away like a sand crab—alone or with me bobbing in tow. But it was clear that socially she wanted nothing to do with Maybelle, whom she saw as the oil to her water.

No—her vinegar.

But three continuous hours of drawing things such as a petrified legless frog in a miniature wheelchair holding pennants that said "Rib" and "Bit!" in either webbed hand just begged for conversation, and Hims took what she could get. Upon realizing that Maybelle's upbringing clearly did not allow for sarcasm, she began to enjoy it.

"I think that frog is Jewish. It's trying to say 'Rabbi.' "

"What?!" Maybelle returned, incredulous.

"Maybe you're right. S'probably Episcopalian— 'Ribeye.' "

• • •

By October Hims insisted I audit her graduate-level Contemporary Art History class because she was tired of having constantly to explain who and what she was talking about.

"You can't possibly enjoy being so ignorant. It's *not* bliss. Bliss is putting a lit match to every fart of Art Dogma this gassy century has seen fit to squeak out. And learning how. Di*vine*."

State's Art History Department actually had a half-decent reputation. AH 401 was taught by Dr. Mistelle, an annoyingly authoritative middle-aged man with a hairless jug head who had published a book on someone called the Blue Rider and spoke and gestured as if he hadn't achieved a successful bowel movement in weeks. Mistelle seemed to know what he was talking about, but his tone implied he had the inside scoop on what each of the artists was trying to do—*whether they realized it or not.*

My AH class, 101, was a tepid introduction to pre-Renaissance painting and sculpture, with a lingering eye on one-point perspective and endless flattened Marys scowling at the fidgets of their dwarfish, petulant savior.

But I'm forever indebted to Hims for making me sit in on 401, as I had no official knowledge of "Modern Art," and without her guidance my introduction to it would have been far more perplexing. During what was to become a pivotal moment for me at

State, Misty put one of the silliest paintings I had ever seen up on the screen. It was of five . . . figures. You could tell that they were supposed to be people because they had eyes. At least three of them were female, sporting pointy boobs the shape of horizontal midget dunce caps. The one farthest to the left apparently started out as a Negro, but the artist changed his mind when he got to the neck and made the rest of her white, pink, apricot, and deep rust.

These she-things looked stunned, as if they'd just been told they all had cervical cancer. And the two on the right were racked with skin problems the likes of which I prayed I'd never know. The whole thing appeared to have been abandoned far from completion, the artist having come to his senses and taken up something less ghastly, like infanticide. Compared to this, Dottie was Picasso.

"This," Mistelle announced, "is Picasso's *Les Damoiselles d'Avignon*. 1907."

Oops.

"After half a century it remains one of the most disturbing paintings in the history of Art. "

Now there he had a point.

"Its convulsive revelation—that the classical nude could attack and transfix the eye at the same time—was unprecedented and has yet to be surpassed. Despite outward appearances to the contrary, its debt to traditional painting is unquestionable. The trio of women on the left form a reference to the Three Graces, a favored theme of the

Renaissance, while the two on the right are a nod to the attenuated forms of El Greco, with a touch of Goya's ferocity. Nonetheless, an undeniable sense of organic unity is achieved through the use of blue, harkening back to, and in transition from, the *misréablisme* of the artist's Blue Period a few years earlier. But he manages to merge it all into a continual membrane of ambiguous declaration—just what is the positive space, and what is the negative? The very problems that Art was traditionally meant to solve are presented here as what they truly are and always have been—problems."

Something strange was happening to me. I was starting to feel ashamed . . .

"If you are shocked by *Les Damoiselles d'Avignon*, that's because it is New, even after fifty years, and anything truly New is always unsettling."

. . . ashamed and stupid.

"This painting," he concluded, "is proof that some new ideas are too fundamental, and too culturally encompassing, to be ignored or dismissed."

I had to admit—as a lawyer for ugly, ham-fisted paintings, Misty was Perry Mason. By the time he was done I was convinced that not only was I an idiot, but this "work" was the product of an unknowable and very real genius.

"Any questions?" Misty always asked this after a tirade, but never meant it. He was really asking, "Can anyone believe how brilliant I am?" Himillsy raised her hand. He reluctantly nodded to her.

"Why is he so afraid of women?" Her tone was civil and intelligent, not blowsy and pronounced like when we'd blab at the Skeller. I came to know that when Mills really wanted to make a point, she could can the Evil Imogene Coca act and present herself seriously.

Misty was dumbfounded. "Picasso? *Afraid* of women? Do you know what you're saying?"

"Look at them. I agree that this is disturbing, but *that's* because so many people fell for it as a serious work. It's a mess."

"I—"

"Why is it some sort of magnificent achievement that Picasso is so threatened by the female form he has to completely debase *it* and basic drawing skills in the process? Why does this demand our attention, much less our *applause*?"

Misty: Scandalized. Then, "Young lady, these women, whatever they are, are not victims."

"Not VICTIMS?" Hims was starting to blow her cool. "Sir, you *must* know that the models for this canvas were five syphilitic prostitutes, and that its original title was *The Avignon Brothel,* subtitled *The Wages of Sin.*"

He recoiled, as if she had just told everyone his bank account number and present balance. Then, he countered: "Which does not necessarily make it an attack."

"No, just the perfect occasion to throw perspective, craft, and respectable draftsmanship out the window," she responded. "If it has anything like a sense of 'organic unity,' it's because this painting has become so familiar it takes on *any* quality we ascribe to it."

He was heating up. "Including the theory that the artist is, absurdly, *frightened* of the female form. Ridiculous."

"Please. The man's a walking castration anxiety. Look at *Seated Bather*. Ask Dora Maar—"

"That's ENOUGH!—" His ears were now perpendicular to his head and the color of a cock's comb. ". . . of this." Debate over. He shot Mills the evil eye and advanced to the next slide. "Let's take a look at *Still Life with Chair Caning* . . . "

• • •

"I've got to stop doing that," said Hims, on our way out of class.

"What."

"Flushing my grades down the toilet."

"But you were fantastic." I tried not to patronize. "When he first put it up on the screen, I thought, 'What a piece of garbage.' But in five seconds he *talked* me into liking it. And I still would, if you hadn't spoken up."

"Thanks, but that probably says more about your gullibility than anything *I* had to say. You can see what we're up against." She slung Baby Laveen over her shoulder. "I don't think Miss Tell will go lightly on my essay answers come the final." She sighed. "And we've *so* much more to slog through. How am I going to button my lip when we get to Matisse? And what if he brings up Pollock and *Rothko*?" She made a face like she was sucking a lime. "Oh, the Truth can be so *expensive*."

We met the cloudless surface world with squints. Mills dug into her bag for her shades.

"Is all their work really *that* bad?" I asked.

"Well, you have to look at things one at a time." Hims clamped her Ray-Bans onto her elfin face. "I've developed a rather brilliant standard—the Grandma Litmus. It's the perfect way to evaluate any work of art—painting, sculpture, what-have-you." She pointed us towards the Creamery and we made tracks. "Now, for Granny Litmus to work, you have to forget anything you know about officially accepted art theory—all the critical stuff, doctrines, movements, museums, and all that, alright?" I nodded. "So: your Grandmother rings you and says she's taken up . . . painting, let's say, and wants you to come over and have a look. So you do, and you go up to the attic of her house and there's a draped canvas. She unveils it and underneath is whatever thing that you want to evaluate. You have to look at it that way, so you can decide."

I didn't get it, and said so.

"In *other* words, Grandma Litmus forces you to remove everything from the context of what these lamebrains call Art History and judge it for what it *is*, not what they *say* it is. You see? Take the Picasso from today—I mean, if Granny painted *that* you'd have her carted off to the happy house."

"Wow, that's pretty . . ."

"Flawless, I believe, is the word you're grasping for. The mistake most people make, when they see something they don't like or can't understand, is to say, 'Christ, my *kid* could do that.' And they sound like Philistines. But if you say, 'Jeez, my Grandmother *did* do that,' it changes everything. Just try it next time you're in a gallery. Imagine that Grandma Litmus painted it or sculpted it or smeared it or flung it or *assembled* it in her spare time and see if it holds up."

"Hmm." I pictured my grandmother in her basement—a gallon bucket of Sherwin-Williams housepaint in one hand and a dripping double-wide brush in the other—standing with triumph in front of one of the De Kooning 'Women' that Misty had just shown us. Yikes. I returned to reality—Himillsy holding open the door to the Creamery.

"God," I said, "but doesn't it cancel out any abstraction at all?"

"No, not if you're honest about it. If my Nanna Dodd painted a . . . Klimt, or a Schiele, or even a Mondrian, I'd slap her on the back and run to call the newspaper."

I'd have to check those names out. I tried to remember the others—the ones she hated. I said,

"It *does* lend a little perspective to . . . to those guys you first mentioned after class."

"Let's just say . . ." She thought for a moment, scanning the flavor board, ". . . that the reports of their depth are *greatly* exaggerated."

• • •

When Mom and Dad arrived to take me home for Thanksgiving, it was almost frightening to see them for the first time after the longest separation we'd ever had. Presto—two vaguely familiar strangers. I wasn't even sure if I should get in the car. Mom, eyes wet and pregnant with joy, held out a round tin, its lid painted with a scene of a pilgrim merrily waving his musket and terrorizing a turkey. "I made peanut butter dates!" As I got in the backseat, all I could concentrate on was the turkey.

I knew exactly how he felt.

"So tell us everything!" was the prevailing theme over the next few days, and I did, almost. Why worry them with talk of things like conspiring to place a pink rubber baby replica in the Alpha Phi rush mixer's punch bowl, or torturing a cat the size of a fire hydrant in the service of Art?

One tidbit I *did* give them: they would have liked Dottie a *lot*.

• • •

During the first week of December, with finals five days away, Himillsy invited me to a Christmas party she and Garnett were throwing in his apartment. I was both eager and wary at the prospect of finally meeting GMG. At last I could pull him into focus, to use as a lens on Miss Dodd—to see her from another angle. But I also had to admit: my self-deluding vanity saw him as . . . the competition.

At five past seven on the appointed Saturday I approached Garnett's building at the west end of town. Mills still lived in the dorms, but Garnett had a place of his own. I couldn't imagine ever being that grown up.

I rang the buzzer. A moment, then the door was cracked, not more than an inch.

"Yes?" A worried female voice.

". . . Himillsy?"

"Oh my God." She opened it the rest of the way. Hims was in her slip, no makeup, half her head in curlers. Manic. "You're an *hour . . . early!*"

"But you said seven."

"Nonsense."

"Sorry, here's the invitation." I pulled it out—her eye-loosening scrawl on the back of an Erbie's receipt. She squinted and held it to her face. Then,

"Well, I was horribly, horribly wrong!"

"Do you want me to come back later?"

"NO!" she screamed, pulling me in. "We're *ages* behind schedule. Here! Chop these!" My coat was grabbed and in exchange two bunches of carrots were magically produced and shoved at me. "Into sticks! And make yourself a drink!" She slammed the bedroom door. A man's muffled voice responded, not happy. She carped back at him. A little more of this, then silence. I made my way to the kitchen—an open extension off the living room, and from there I took a look around. There was no bar, anywhere, that I could see.

So I drank in the space.

And wow, it went down like no slurp 'n' burp ever would. It wasn't lavish, not in the way I knew the word, but it was . . . organized. And stark. A single large poster, the only "art" of any kind, lorded over the room—it was a white field with a jagged black line running from top to bottom down the center, with a black square off to its upper left. At the base, in plain black lettering, it said BAUHAUS. Some other information, smaller, in what I supposed was German, was sprinkled underneath. After a few seconds, its random shapes assembled themselves in my mind and became the extremely abstracted right-hand profile of a man's head.

The furniture was in varying combinations of black leather, glass, and chrome. The floors, wooden, were painted white, as were the walls and ceiling. The proportions were exact—you felt that if anything strayed so much as an inch the whole place would self-destruct. The chairs (they *had* to be chairs) were at a respectful distance from the coffee table, the couch, each other. This wasn't a revelation by itself, but something made it special. Or rather, some burden had been lifted. I looked for a paper towel to wipe the carrot dirt off my hands. There weren't any.

But of course: no clutter. No newspapers, no renegade scraps of domestic detritus, no rubber bands, paper clips, coupons, pens or pencils, notebooks, magazines. No knives. Where were the knives?

I turned to the kitchen cabinets. Where were the *knobs*?

This was the Un-dorm.

I fumbled with the lower edges of the ghost-white doors. I begged, I pulled, and I coaxed. Were there secret latches, catches, buttons, hidden levers? Nothing. And in the process I left a doodle of dirt from the carrots. I pulled out my shirttail to wipe it away, but most of the marks were too high up. I gingerly climbed onto the counter and unbuttoned my two lowest shirt buttons in order to reach them and—

"Is everything alright?" Himillsy's voice. I got down and turned. My God. Not Himillsy. This was a . . . woman. Her black satin off-the-shoulder sheath became a stiletto that cleaved the floor with each step. Pure Gertrude Lawrence, as sharp and smart as a Noël Coward lyric.

"I. I can't *open* anything," I said, miserably.

"Oh, I *know*," she sneered, "Garnett *designed* it

all. The apartment is his graduate thesis. Workmen finally left last week." She made her way into the kitchen, gave one of the drawers a light tap, right in the middle, and it magically popped open. Ta-da. Cutlery.

Her lids at half mast, her eyes to the ceiling: "Welcome to Utopia."

Once we had the crudités all set Hims picked up the tray and said, "Give me a hand with the other hors d'oeuvre?— in the fridge."

"Sure." I opened it and removed a plate with rolls of dried beef and cream cheese impaled on toothpicks. She went to the nearest living room window, balanced the tray on one knee, threw up the sash, and waited for me to follow. "Where're we going?" I asked, as she was halfway through.

"Fire escape." Which was big—a terrace, really, made of latticed wrought iron. We set the food on a metal folding table covered with a white tablecloth and already set with punch bowl, glasses, napkins, plates, the whole nine. Brisk out there. We rushed back in.

"What'll you have?" She opened a panel under the counter that slid out to reveal an entire bar set.

"Wow, that's pretty great, actually. Um, a whiskey sour?"

She removed a cocktail shaker and several long-stem glasses. "We're not at Phi *Sig*, let's have martinis!"

"Okay. What's with the table?" I gestured towards the window.

"That's where the party is."

"Out *there*?"

"House rules. No food inside. Not till after dissertation, anyway."

"Why have a party at all?"

Surprised at me. Mock shock. "What? How often does a virgin give *birth*?" She shook the cocktails into oblivion. On the level: "Actually, quite smart on G's part—a little sneak peak for the cognoscenti—good third of the guests'll be Ark faculty, the rest grad students and a few seniors. Let 'em lift the skirt and have a look."

"You starting *already*?" A man's voice—cutting enough to carve a date into a cornerstone. I pivoted.

He put out his hand.

"Garnett Grey."

Yes, Garnett Grey was an Architect. Were a psychoanalyst to approach him from behind, tap his shoulder, and say "Humanity," Garnett'd spin and respond, without hesitation, "Solvable."

Not conventionally attractive, but Grey was so self-constructed he became handsome because you knew he was supposed to be—like when you bought it that Superman was flying on TV even though you could see the wires.

"Dodd tells me you're a freshman. Welcome aboard." He said it as if he'd just hired me, entry level.

"Thanks."

Hims cringed. "Ahoy."

The guests started to arrive, and after thirty minutes I could have sworn I was in the first draft of an Ayn Rand novel. That this little pocket of proto-aesthetes really existed in State's Disneyland of academic banality was more than I could have expected, let alone hoped to get a load of. A stroll down the hallway outside the living room put me under a confetti shower of conversational bits from the Erector Set, all above and beyond me.

" . . . the surfaces, the *surfaces* . . . "

" . . . related to Eileen Gray? The spelling's different . . . "

" . . . ornamental folly. *Never* get tenure. Refill? . . . "

" . . . ever *seen* Lever House? Change your *life*..."

" . . . Neutra's the future. I'll have another egg nog . . . "

" . . . trip to Falling Water this weekend. You *going*? . . . "

" . . . Eames? *Tinker* toys. No more for me, thanks . . . "

" . . . Phillip Johnson should *never* throw stones . . . "

" . . . its Broyer, not *Brewer*. Where's the *tree*? . . . "

" . . . he's already got an offer from Skidmore . . . "

" . . . site specific? Try a garbage dump . . . "

Everyone wore black or white or a shade in

between. Were it not for the temperature outside, you'd never know what the occasion was. Not a red or green anything in sight.

On the way to pee, I couldn't resist stealing a peek into Garnett's bedroom—aha!—an absolute wreck. The Clutter Inferno: a scandalous heap of clothes, books, papers, and underthings. From what I could tell, all Himillsy's. It was the living room's dark alter ego of upheaval. What a relief.

At around eleven I chanced upon a woman in a Moe-of-the-Three Stooges hairdo and face to match. She was stuffed into a short leather skirt (which she did NOT have the legs for), and ran her hand across the kitchen cabinets like a blind man going over a Brancusi. "An astonishment, really. Corbu couldn't have done better."

Garnett beamed. Or did his version of it, anyway: a stony, focused scowl.

"That's because Corbusier is a blockhead, in more ways than one." Himillsy eased into the kitchen, steady but on the other side of sober. "Half his Human Storage Boxes are falling apart already." Her tongue: ready to open oysters.

Miss Moe-thuzelah: scandalized.

Garnett looked at Mills the way the Empire State building would regard the corner deli. "Dodd, Le Corbusier is not being judged."

Hims: seething, muted. "Well. Excuse the piss

out of *me*. Switched your major to Drama?" She went to the sill, paused on her way to the balcony—one leg in, one leg out—and hissed, "Less is a bore."

I followed her through the window, stunned by the realization that I'd have done so balcony or no. Outside it was even colder now, though after a while (and enough liquid insulation) you didn't notice it.

"Look at that." She waved her cigarette back at her enemies. "That's a living room for the dead. A Venusian sculpture garden. Everyone's either in the hallway or out here." Which was only us, actually. Then she grinned, horribly. "Have you seen the bedroom?"

"Have, sorry." I moved in next to her, wanting to understand, to advance to . . . I don't know, the next level with her. "I . . . don't get you. You go on about how modernism is crap, but you're definitely a creature *of* it. It's hard to really tell *what* you are."

"That's because, I'm not much of anything," she stiffened and took another sip and leaned on the railing, "besides bored and boring, punctuated by fits of scant self-amusement. And you are . . . ?"

"Protestant." I wanted to say so, so much more. Pathetic.

She clinked my drink. "Jingle all the way."

"You're *not* boring." I implored, "God, if *you're* boring then the rest of us are pushing up daisies."

"Everything's relative."

A lull. Watched our breath bloom and disappear.

And then she started, as if she were sober, "Look," and confessing, after a long interrogation. I went hot all over—was she going to say something about me? About what I meant to her? "Those buildings, the first ones, that Gropius did, were . . . unlike anything before them . . . but more important, they spoke to a need for clarity and honest precision that no one had been able to achieve—or, before the twentieth century—even thought to." A sigh. "To be in one—the Fagus Shoe Last factory in 1911, for the first time—it must have truly sung to the soul and rewarded a spark of true faith in the promise of a, a new ideal. Christ knows the rest of Germany didn't." She receded into a theater of her own expectation, adoring, then her face fell. "Only to have the floor fall out from under their kneeling legs. The problem is there's a difference between revolutionary minimalism and substituting archival stone with poured concrete that starts to crack before the first photo session is over. In short, the Bauhaus opened the floodgates to a worldwide generation of hacks who decided that details, structural quality, and solid craft were options they didn't need to opt for. That wasn't the intent, I realize," she scoped out the table for a bottle, "but we all know what they say about good intentions . . ."

Or *any* intentions. What an idiot I was. "Yes . . . ," I offered, weakly. I'd digested very little of what all that was about, except for this: it was rehearsed. If I had any doubts left about what she was doing with someone like Garnett, she just erased them. She needed a worthy foe, always—someone to charge and ricochet off of in order to keep up the momentum. And I would never, could never, be that. Garnett was fuel for her. To burn.

And lucky him: he seemed to be lined with asbestos.

"Oh, that reminds me, Piggy Sutton told me a real oner in Miss Tell's today." She poured herself more gin, coming back to life. "How many Surrealists does it take to change a lightbulb?"

"I give."

"Fish!" She was joyous.

I didn't get it. I didn't get anything. Of course I broke up anyway.

"Isn't that a panic?"

A stern voice sliced through our laughter.

"H, you're tighter than a snare drum." Garnett, arms extended, leaned out the window and made me eight years old again, caught red-handed in Mr. McGlynn's backyard taking a whiz in the azaleas.

Hims looked at him. Her face held all the blackness of a Goya sky on the Third of May.

"If I throw a stick," she spat, hanging her head, "will you *leave*?"

• • •

WINTER BREAK

When we pause, amidst the Yuletide festivities, to reflect upon that which we have learned so far, and look eagerly towards what's to come.

C R E D I T S : o

And so onto Christmas, when thoughts turned to good will towards men, the miracle of the manger, and at our house, Manhattans with six cherries as we gathered around the piano. At which point Dad, Uncle Joey, and I would carefully lift it up and struggle to move it to the other side of the den.

"See? The room's bigger already!" cheered Aunt Sophie, who saw holidays primarily as something of a Divine Mandate to get loaded and rearrange our furniture. "Just needed to get it out of the corner! Took! Where's my drink?"

"Not sure, Soph," Mom lied. I fetched it from the piano stool and handed it to her. Mom shot me a poisonous look and went into the kitchen to finish shellacking the swollen ham with Karo syrup. Aunt Sophie drained her glass in a gulp—with Mom out of the room, the mice could play. They were sisters, and Soph was the Margaret Hamilton to Mom's Billie Burke—except that liquids didn't destroy her, they made her stronger.

"C'mon, Dom!" she said to Dad, sneaking to the bar, "just a halvsie!"

Dad was largely powerless to resist her, because she acted on every impulse he would himself have succumbed to if he thought he had permission. They refilled their drinks.

"I'm an alco*frolic*, there's a *difference*!"

I was in a pretty good mood, for several reasons. First, I was finally allowed to drink at home, and quickly learned how to do it without ending the evening crouched over a toilet and waking up the next day in tears. Second, I was confident that I had aced my first term's finals. Third, Vermont was initiated into AGR and out of 613—bringing my restless nights in the garret to an end. The only thing missing was Himillsy. If only she could be here to expose how dopey it all was, we could get blotto and laugh at everything.

"That side table has got to go!" Aunt Sophie started to clear the faux teak wood postcolonial number that commanded the center of the den. "Dom, how many times have I told her? C'mon, let's just see what would happen if it disappeared." That was our cue to move it to the carport. Mom would explode, but regardless (or just maybe because of), Dad and I picked it up with the gravity of pallbearers. We were halfway there when the doorbell rang. On Christmas Eve?

"Took, is that the Reardons?" shouted Aunt Sophie. "If it is, we're not here. They're *shafers*!" That was her term for anybody or anything unacceptable.

"What?" Mom wailed from the kitchen, "Soph! Whoever it is, c'mon in! Merry Christmas!"

I went to the door. It was a UPS worker, holding a box.

"Hi there,"

"Special delivery. Sign here, please." I took it in. The return address read H. Dodd Industries, Inc. Guilford, Conn.

Holy shit.

Mom: "What is it dear?"

"Uh, it's a present, I think, for me."

"Wow! Who's it from, hon?"

"A friend from school. A girl."

She ran down the steps and into the den. "You met a *girl*? Why didn't you *tell* us? Where is she?"

"Mom, she's at home, in Connecticut. This is just something she sent me. It's not like that."

She looked around the room, puzzled.

"Where's the end table? Soph!" Turning red. "Now that's *enough*! It's from Wanamakers! Dom, put it back."

"Oh Took," Aunt Sophie was practically speaking in tongues, "it's *shafers*! Look! The den's so *open* now. Don't you think? Live with it till New Year's. You'll *thank* me, you'll see . . ."

Mom, who had the whole rest of the holidays to cruise direct, said "Oh, I give up," and went back to the kitchen.

"So, let's see what's cookin'!" Aunt Sophie eyed the box, ravenous for experience.

"Yeah!" said Uncle Joey, "Whadja get from Connecticut?"

"Um, shouldn't I wait till tomorrow?"

"Hell, we'll be at MaryBeth's. Here, let me get you another stinger." She ran to the bar with my glass, bless her.

"Thanks." I sat in the Barcalounger and started to unwrap it. Craft paper gave way to cardboard. I opened the flaps, and there was . . .

Baby Laveen. In swaddling clothes. With a noisemaker in his mouth made out of pages from the New Testament. He lay in a bed of at least two dozen shriveled balloons, half deflated, that said "Happy Birthday!" A halo made out of a glitter-covered wire clothes hanger—anchored in his back and suspended over his head, and there were . . . stigmata on his hands and feet. He was clutching a sign that said, "No VACANCY?! I want to see the MANAGER!! Don't you know who I AM?! No, not MANGER, I said—"

I closed it up, pronto.

"Well, what is it? Here." She handed me my glass.

"Thanks. Actually . . . it's not a present. Just some books I needed, for winter break. Nothing special." I got up to take it to my room, my heart warm with the meaning of Christmas.

"Books? That's *shafers!*"

• • •

The Diner: second week of January. Our booth and *God* it was great to see her again. I checked my impulse to say something sappy and lifted Savior Laveen from his manger box with care. Hims had put in a note saying that he was strictly on loan to bring holiday cheer, and come the new term he was to ascend back into her realm. I was flattered to be entrusted with such a cosmic responsibility.

"So well be*haved*," I remarked, returning Him to her arms. "Fixed Grandma's eyesight, made her walk again. Wouldn't take a *dime*."

She giggled. "What did Mamá make of him?"

"You kidding? Thank God I opened it first."

"I should have addressed it to *her*."

"How did you know where to send it?"

"Information, natch. I hope you held Him high when Tiberius did the head count."

"Wanted to, but the Wiseguys showed up a week late and hogged all his time. So *pushy*." Yuckety yuck. "So what's on the agenda this term?" Classes started in five days.

"Oh, who cares? Art History 425, probably—Cathedrals. Fourth-level French. Quoits. The usual."

"No studio classes?" Not taking *some*thing with her was just beyond bearing.

"Sure. We'll see."

During a frigid Sunday afternoon stroll that weekend down the Mall (the main thoroughfare on campus, lined with a hallway of oaks that ran from the town line up to the library), Hims pushed Baby Laveen in the magnificent stainless steel streamlined art deco stroller she'd found at the Salvation Army for three dollars. I followed alongside and couldn't help but grin—our happy little family. "Hey, watch this!" she suddenly whispered, as a woman approached from about forty feet away. Hims stopped and leaned down to Baby Laveen.

"Smile, darling!" she sang to her charge. The woman, charmed, continued towards us.

"Come on, my little cheese monkey. A smile for Mummy!" she pinched his tiny polymer cheek. Footsteps, louder.

"I said SMILE!" She stood up and gave the stroller a mighty kick. The wheels rattled with a steely clang as it spun away in a forty-five-degree pivot and knocked into the heavily initialed trunk of one of the trees. The woman, shaken, pulled up her coat collar around her gaping mouth and rushed past. Hims turned to me and announced, with the brightness of an H-bomb,

"Look, honey, he's *smiling*!"

•••

Maybelle begged me to register for spring classes with her and I couldn't think of a tactful way to say no. Determined to learn from our Dantean experience of the fall, I said to meet me at eight, southwest corner of the Burser's. Foiled: so did everyone else. Found her by eight-thirty.

The same turmoil as last time, only colder outside. Was Hims among the throng? Didn't see her. Two hours later, in the Burser's with only three more kids ahead of us, a familiar voice rose from the discord.

"Darleeeengs! Woo-hoo!!" Himillsy parted the agitated multitude like Moses and sidled up to us, leaving a wake of angry, angry stares.

"One side! Whew! What a *rhubarb*! Am I too late?"

Amazing: I conjured her.

"Just in time, sugar!" Maybelle hollered. "We're just about to go!" She prodded me. "I think he should do it for all of us, he's so good!"

"Swell!"

We devised a strategy of choices, and in ten minutes, it was our turn.

Behind the Registrar's window #6 sat a jowlish brunette in her late forties with a jones for Mary-Janes and hairpins. "Audry" was stenciled on her nametag. Not easy on the eyes—compared to Audry, Nikita Khrushchev was an airline hostess. At least she didn't tell us we were in the wrong line.

Maybelle and Hims handed me their registration sheets, filled out sans Art classes. We got through all of the nonelectives, then,

"Alright, Studio requirements."

"Great."

Hims egged me on. "Hit one into the bleachers, slugger."

I leaned into the slotted circular aluminum opening. "Drawing two-oh-one, please. For three." She riffled her papers.

"Filled, dear." Rats. I opened the catalog.

"Two-oh-two?"

"Same."

Scanning a page. "How about Painting One-oh-three?"

"Sorry."

"Color Theory?"

" 'Fraid not."

Flipflipflip."Intro to Life Drawing?"

"Umm. No."

Shit. I pulled out my emergency list—scrawled last night onto a Baby Ruth wrapper. "Advanced Life Drawing?"

"Let's see now . . . no, dear."

"Death Drawing?"

"*What?*"

"Kidding, sorry. Intermediate Still Life?"

"Oh isn't this *awful* . . . no, nope."

"Light and Landscape."

"Just closed."

"Perspective and—"

"Goes fast—"

"Lord love a DUCK!! WHAT'S OPEN?!" I don't, usually, ever lose my temper. Audry unwrapped a piece of the peanut taffy and poked it into her mouth.

"My, goodness. Aren't *we* being . . ." She licked her fingers and surveyed her papers. "Let's see . . . Oh! There's a *new* class they just added, not even in the *catalog*. New teacher, too. A Miss . . . Sorbeck. Art One-twenty-seven: Introduction to Commercial Art."

Hims sneered. "Sign painting? Forget it."

"*You* find an alternative," I said. She rustled through her bag and pulled out her compact, pretending she didn't hear me—giving in and saving face.

"Sounds good, *I* think," said Maybelle. "Couldn't hurt to have a few practical skills, right?"

"Three slots?" I asked Audry.

"Yep, just."

"Sign us up."

• • •

SPRING SEMESTER

1958

ART 127. INTRODUCTION TO COMMERCIAL ART.

INSTR.: PROF. W. SORBECK, BFA
Tues. & Thurs., 2:25 p.m.

ROOM 207, BAXTER BLDG.
(FORMERLY WEXLER SCIENCE HALL)

DESCR: A fundamental exploration
of the applied arts.

CREDITS: 3

I got there at quarter past two. A dozen or so kids dotted the benches and floor in the hall facing the classroom—I recognized Treat Dempsey and two other guys from North Halls. Himillsy was seated, her shiny black helmet of hair and raccoon mascara glowering over a sundress she'd made in Textiles 202. The fabric was covered with a pattern of oranges and bananas that would have seemed perfectly benign on anyone else. She was talking to a very tall boyish man with terrible skin. The door to 207 wasn't locked, but a sign, ink on horizontal notebook paper, was taped to it:

INTRODUCTION TO <u>GRAPHIC</u> <u>DESIGN</u>
Formerly mislabeled
INTRODUCTION TO COMMERCIAL ART

ENTER THE CLASSROOM AT <u>EXACTLY</u>
2:25 P.M. —WS

"I think you should go in."

Hims was smirking, sunbeam bright. I recognized the look and prepared myself—it was the sort of smile that made you check your fly. Suddenly she was nudging me to the door, giddy with girlish urgency—I was Rin Tin Tin and she lay pinned under a tree. "Go on, hurry! Don't think about me! Run! Save your*self*!"

I resisted, with success. "Rage before beauty ..." I held one arm to my chest and extended the other towards the door. She returned a howl of delighted disapproval and slid over to make space for me on the bench.

"This is Mike," she gestured vaguely to the beanpole, who, now that I was seated, seemed even longer and lankier. Mike Crenck was ancient—maybe even thirty. As he nodded my way and made a small noise, the expression on his face made me want to say "Don't worry, I'm not going to hurt you." His hair was sandy colored, in a shade which reminded you that sand was also dirt.

"What are y'all waiting for?" Maybelle was at the far end of the hallway, lugging her burden of paints, pencils, rulers, and drawing tools—charging towards us with epic resolve. Only Mabes could turn walking down the hall into Lee's campaign at Gettysburg.

"For you. Go on in." Mills was swinging her legs.

Maybelle ignored her and read the sign. "Well. Miss Sorbeck is very specific, isn't she?"

"Probably moonlights as a Swiss cuckoo," said Hims, as she tortured a paper clip.

I sighed and leaned against the wall. What a bore this was going to be, like every other class at State. At least I talked Mills into taking it. She'd liven it up.

At twenty-five after, we made our listless way into 207 and found seats. A minute or two of silence.

Then, from behind us:

"That was *lousy.* Do it again."

It is beyond my powers to tell you what that voice really sounded like. But I can tell you what it did. I *can* say it pinned me like a Monarch to its specimen box and made me squint. It turned the air into a hot solid. Wait—that's not good enough—it . . . was a wave you thought you could ride, until you did, and came up bloody. I can tell you it was the sound of Ultimate Discontent—the voice that, after a long life of committing horrible crimes, you could expect to hear just after you died.

I turned, opened my eyes.

There, leaning against the back wall, was Gary Cooper's fraternal twin (*High Noon*-era) in a white dress shirt and loosened rep tie, gray flannel trousers, and a pipe driven into his clenched teeth.

But I bet Gary never forgave him because between the two this guy got all the looks—which were now on the other side of Stellar—but not far. He was big. Not fat, not at all. Big. Like a cliff you were just pushed from.

To look at him was to disappoint him.

"I said. Do it. Again."

And boy, did we ever.

We rose with a collective jolt, filed out into the hallway, and exchanged puzzled glances. What to do next?

"There must be some mistake," offered Maybelle. "He must think we're here for something else. Maybe he's not the right teacher at all. Once at Miss Cress's I spent an entire term in Pillows when I was supposed to be in Napkins. I almost didn't graduate. It was just *crazy*."

Treat and the two he came with were heading down the hall for the stairwell. I called to him.

"Where're you guys going?"

He turned. "To see if we can still audit Psych One-ten." Then he shot a wild-eyed face to the door of 207 and they were gone.

Hims was jubilant—fortified by the weirdness and confusion. "*Love* it! Kicked out already and we didn't even do anything. Let's go back in!"

"But we did it wrong somehow last time." Maybelle bit her lip. "What did he mean?"

"He means do it with some *style*," said Mills. "Go in like . . . oh . . . *Isadora Duncan*."

"Who?"

"Jesus. *Agnes de Mille*, then."

"I don't—"

"Like a dancer in *Oklahoma*. Go ahead. Kick up your heels. He'll love it. We'll be right behind you."

"Are you sure?" She pondered it. "I loved *Oklahoma*, saw it three times. They had such spirit, those poor people. Do you *think* . . . ?"

"Absolutely. He wants theater. I'm going to be Blind Pew from *Treasure Island*. I'll use my ruler as a tapping stick. Be fun!" She turned to me. "What are you going to be?"

In eternally horrified thrall to you, alas. "I'm still deciding." Everyone else had started to go back in, some with a little more enthusiasm than before. Maybelle bounded into the room, clicked her heels, and shouted, "Yeeeeah!!"

Sorbeck was stone-faced. Himillsy followed her up and gave him a very desperate, apologetic glance. I was next, and before I sat down, something came over me and I pivoted, clicked my heels together, and did a slow, courtly bow.

Arms crossed. Didn't move.

Once we were all reseated, he went to the front of the room and started bobbing his head at each of us. Then,

"Shit. Only three went AWOL?"

Mike raised his hand and said in a voice that sounded like Bing Crosby before puberty. "I, I think so."

And then, *bam!* The first of his magical transformations: now a human being—almost friendly. "I must be losing my touch." He smiled and turned the air into a gas again and became the most beguiling person on earth. "Usually it's at least five. I'll have to work on that. You see, there's still eighteen people here. The class works better with twelve, best with fewer. Nine or ten is ideal. Of course, the Cookie Cutters in the front office of this Idiot Factory won't allow me to limit it to that, but I'm not worried. I'll whittle you down. No doubts."

I didn't like the sound of that.

"Before we go on, I should state, it's a fact: Nothing worth knowing can ever be taught in a classroom."

No one stirred.

"Well. Nobody fell for *that.* Now. Let's see what we've got." He walked across the front of the room, and I was reminded of a shark I once saw during a high school field trip—it was turning in a tank of cloudy water, and I just kept staring at it, thinking, *"How can something so huge and bulky move with such efficient, liquid ease?"* Its fin broke the surface and bore down—Christ—on *me*. "Son, what is the name of this class?"

His face: the Arrow shirt man after some hard, hard years.

Survivalist reflexes almost made me shriek "Introduction to Commercial Art!" Almost. At the last second I remembered the sign. I cleared my throat. "Introduction to Graphic Desi—"

"RIGHT!!" God. "Very good. You can stay. For now." Maybelle was next. "Honey, can you tell me what Graphic Design is?"

She thought for a moment. "No. I'm afraid not," all eager smiles. "That's why I'm here, I suppose."

He seemed to accept that. "All right. Fair enough, you're in."

Back to Mike. Sorbeck folded his arms and leaned down on the table. "What does the world look like?"

"Er, I don't think I understand the question."

"Now, *that* is a problem." He stood up and reloaded his pipe. "That *is* a problem.

"Everyone, understand: When you walk through that door you become a graphic designer. Whether or not you stay one after you leave is up to you, but I'd recommend you wear the mantle full time, all semester. We'll be spending the next weeks attempting to figure out what this means—to be a designer, graphic or otherwise.

"Now who would like to take a little eye test? You two." He gestured to Himillsy and the girl next to her—a real Margaret-from-Dennis-the-Menace type, with freckles and rust-colored ringlets propped up by two pink barrettes shaped like butterflies. "Up to the front of the room please, and face the class." Hims rolled her eyes as she passed me.

Then he said, serious as a cancer: "Okay, I want you ladies to close your eyes. NO peeking or out the door with you both. I'm watching. Understand?" They did as they were told and nodded. "Alright, we'll start with the pigtails. Sweetheart?"

"Yes?" said Margaret.

"What color is the floor?"

"Uh." She started to look down, and checked herself. Lids clenched tight. "I really, couldn't say for sure."

"I see. How about the walls?"

"Oh. I. Didn't get a good look at them. Green?"

"Hmm. How many windows are in this room?"

"Gee. I . . . didn't count."

"Describe the dress of the girl next to you."

"Uh, orange." Very fidgety.

"Her shoes."

Silence.

"*My* shoes. What color?"

"Brown?"

Hims had her hands clasped behind her through all of this, her tiny weight on her left leg. Smiling. Head tilted to the ceiling. Bored, bored, bored.

"Pigtails, we have to teach you how to *see*. Either that or get you a tapping stick and a dog with a metal handle and a *lot* of patience." Titters in the room. Then, quite grave: "You are a *designer*. You have to *eat* the world with your eyes. You must look at everything as if you're going to die in the next five minutes, because in the relative scheme of things, you are. You can't miss a trick. Now, you, girly." He meant Himillsy. "In the fruit dress. What colo—"

"The floor, originally I suppose, was white. As one would like to imagine that slush in the gutter was once new-fallen snow. Linoleum. Of the grade . . . usually found in Sears just before they remodeled. Scuffed now, beyond redemption." She smirked slightly, into the dark.

"Well well well." His interest was finally sparked—the badger at the rabbit hole. "Go on."

"The walls are the shade of caked snot."

He said nothing.

"Cinder block. There are either four windows or eight, depending on whether you count them in sections. Probably last washed during the Roosevelt administration. Teddy." She was off and running—arms up into space. "I'm wearing my own stunning creation—I call it 'Fruit Salad Surgery.' My shoes are boys' size four patent black leather Buster Browns with kid straps." She threw her hands crazily to the right. "Miss *Nowhere* is wearing a thigh-waisted fatigue tent-dress she probably made in her spare time to save money for hair dye."

Margaret's eyes snapped open.

"—speaking of which, someone might tell her that two killer moths the color of my tongue are attacking her head as I speak."

"Hey!"

"And you, sir, since you asked, are shod in a pair of groaning black ox-bloods that really ought to be thrown away. You obviously aren't married, or Mrs. Sorbeck would have returned them apologetically to the beast they were ripped from, when you weren't looking, years ago."

He chuckled. "Oh, she tried. I'm *always* looking. And?"

"I'm *stuffed*." She opened her lids. "My eyeballs are ready to burp their heads off." She curtsied and headed for her seat. Margaret followed in a slump. I pictured those wavy cartoon heat lines rising from her head, and almost started to clap.

Sorbeck was as amused as I ever would see him. Sober, anyway.

"You're a *pip*, Miss Molecule."

She basked in the praise.

"Kiddies, you all should have been able to do that. Sans, I would hope," he threw a second's dismissive glance at Himillsy, "the undergraduate humor."

Hims's face broke and she made her eyes dark slits. She didn't like that. Not at *all*.

"The Cookie Cutters can't think about anything beyond selling cookies, so they would have you believe this class is the Introduction to Commercial Art. It is not. Should that give you cause to leave this room, do so now—without the threat of being scorned, or having to think."

Nobody did. Leave, I mean.

"But I've been put in charge of the store here, and I say it's Introduction to Graphic Design. The difference is as crucial as it is enormous—as important as the difference between pre- and postwar America. Uncle Sam . . . is Commercial Art. The American Flag is Graphic Design. Commercial Art tries to make you *buy* things. Graphic Design *gives* you ideas. One natters on and on, the other actually has something to say. They use the same tools—words, pictures, colors. The difference, as you'll be seeing, and as you'll be showing me, is *how*." He bowed his head and paused, as if to take on a new load of thoughts. Then he paced, slowly, up and down the right side of the room.

"You're lucky. I envy you—this is an interesting time for Graphic Design. Even though it's existed since the dawn of man, it's also in its infancy—not even a name for it until 1928, when a book designer named William Addison Dwiggins got sick of the term 'Graphic Arts' and changed it—in print, naturally. And he was right. It's not Art. And Art is not Design, though it used to be." He stopped, relit his pipe. Drew it in.

"Design is, literally, purposeful planning. Graphic Design, then, is the form those plans will take."

More thoughts.

"A bazillion years ago, some poor son of a bitch Cro-Magnon scratched a drawing of a buffalo onto the wall of his cave. He didn't do it because his *muse* had *called* to him, or to explore the texture of bauxite, or to start the neoprimitive-expressionist movement. He did it because he killed a goddamn buffalo and he wanted someone else to know about it, *after he was gone.* He had a specific, definable purpose for making a piece of visual information. The first one." He puffed. "Whether it's been up or downhill from there is a matter of debate for another time, but the truth is Art and Design only finally parted ways in the nineteenth century, with the introduction of photography. Now—*Ssmile!*—Zogg can take a *picture* of his Buffalo and save all those tedious drafting skills for . . . well, something else."

Sorbeck pulled a chair up to the front, sat, and propped his legs up on a desk, leaning back, hands behind his head.

"Which is no small matter. You see, photography opened up quite a little Pandora's box, kiddies. Do you have any *idea*?" A quick scan of the room made it clear we didn't. "Once we no longer had to depend on drawing and painting to record our existence—once they became an *option*—they mutated . . . into a form of *expression*. And Art for its own sake, God help us, was born.

"But Graphic Design for its own sake will never happen, because the concept cancels itself out—a poster about nothing other than itself is *not* Graphic Design, it's . . ." He pumped his fist rapidly up and down over his lap and started breathing in spasms. ". . . *makin' ART*."

My goodness.

"Not that Design can't have . . . a look, a *style*—in fact it has to, even if the style is 'no style'—but by definition, Design must always be in service to solving a problem, or it's not Design. I will not, so help me, ever attempt to define what Art is. But I know what it no longer is, and that's Graphic Design.

"Now, as for Commercial Art, I could be crass and say the term is both repetitive and redundant, but that's too easy. Better to say the term is too limiting and too humiliating. I mean, do you really want to be a *Commercial Artist*?" He somehow made his face ugly with those last two words, for just a second, then stood. Summing up his case.

"Eight notes in the scale: you can write either 'Smoke Gets In Your Eyes' or *The Marriage of Figaro*.

"Twenty-six letters: *Marjorie Morningstar* or *Ulysses*.

"The man-made world means exactly that. There isn't an inch of it that doesn't have to be dealt with, figured out, executed. And it's waiting for you to decide what it's going to look like. Of course that's not true, but for this class you have to believe it.

"So. Is it caked snot?

"Or five coats of lacquered enamel?"

We didn't dare make a peep. I was exhausted just listening.

"Alright. Here's your first assignment . . ."

. . .

"I wish I had a picture of him. Then my word could be 'bastard.' Problem *solved*." Himillsy was burrowing through her purse, her last Camel hanging from her mouth for dear life. "Bloody *matches . . .*"

For our first formal Graphic Design critique we had to select a word and design it, on an eleven-by-fourteen-inch piece of paper. The idea was to make it look appropriate to what it said. Sounds simple enough, until you try it—everything you think of is instant cliché. Himillsy and I met at Zingorelli's Pizza—their tomato-garlic strombolis could set off Vesuvius—the night before it was due, to commiserate.

"How about the word 'red,' in red?" I asked.

"Too easy. He'll hate it. *There* they are . . ." Breath a Sicilian stink bomb, she lit her smoke and motioned for her sixth Coke. "Plus like he said—it's too repetitive. He's looking for more."

A truck pulled up and parked on the curb outside the window next to our booth. It was huge. Lost in thought, I found myself trying to read the lettering on the side, but only part of it was in view, and all I could make out, just barely, was the word 'big.' Hmm. Now *there* was an idea.

Was *this* Design? Taking the information on

the side of that truck, and seeing not what it is, but what could be made of it? Learning from it?

I decided yes. It was that moment—when the mind, instead of obsessively pacing the prison of its own puzzlement, suddenly, instinctively, deliriously, discovers a way to make wings out of wax and fly the maze.

"What if the word was 'big' . . . " I started, "but you just showed a white piece of paper?"

She waited for me to explain. I said, "Because it's so big, you can't see it all."

She took a drag. "Interesting, but something about it . . . isn't right." Sent smoke to the ceiling. "I wouldn't if I were you." Dissmissal Herself.

Ouch. Moment: RIP. "Yeah, I guess. What's everybody else doing?"

A foreign concept. "What? Who *cares*?" Himillsy's camaraderie was often cut with a sense of narcissism that was scarcely less than monstrous.

"That one guy, Mike," I said, "he's been working on it for two nights, in the Belly." (The Visual Arts building's basement workroom, where you went when you really needed to spread out. When you needed *surfaces*.) I already suspected that Mike was going to be one of those humble show-off types who worked harder than everybody else on each project and became teacher's pet. Annoying.

"Pizza Face?" she sniffed. "Bully for him. Vote him Class Prez."

"Maybe I should try a noun. What are you going to do?"

"Skip class."

"Seriously."

"Oh I don't know. I'll do what I always do." She drained her glass, stubbed out her Camel's tail. We got up to leave. "I'll think of something at the last minute. Drop you?"

. . .

BASIC INTERLUDE (1)

Morning.

Today we are going to talk about Left to Right. If I thought that I could say, "Things go from left to right," and all of you would grasp the weight of the situation then I would just say it and that would be that and we could just go home for today because, really, that's enough. No, too much for one day, actually. The best way would be to say, "Things go from left" on Tuesday, let it sink in, and then say "to right" on Thursday. And you know how you'd picture it? You'd picture Tuesday on the left, and Thursday on the right, and we'd be all set. In fact, why the hell didn't I do that? Damn. Too late. Anyway, that would assume this circumstance doesn't require some explanation, and as I survey this room, it's clear to me it does.

Look. Suppose you were a general in battle someplace and you got wind the enemy was plotting to invade your territory. If you knew exactly ahead of time where the sonsabitches were going to land and strike, you'd have the advantage, right? Well, that's it. You, you all have the advantage. The page, the poster, the surface you are working on—THAT'S your territory, and they are going to invade. Fine, let them. That's what you want anyway. But be ready.

They are coming in from the left. Always, always always, always!! This, as you would imagine, can be extremely useful to know. For example, if the director of a play wants to give more importance to one character than the others, where do you think he's going to place him on stage? See? You invisibly assign a hierarchy of importance and meaning to the elements you work with by deciding where they go on the page.

We are the Western world. We read, see, think. Left. To. Right. We can't help it. You have few givens in this life, in this class. That is one of them. Use it.

THE FIRST CRITIQUE.

In Art 127 (Introduction to Graphic Design),
W. Sorbeck, instr.

Our task: Choose a word and then design it with the
typography and materials of our choice, on a piece of
paper 11" x 14", to be viewed vertically or horizon-
tally.

Give the word appropriate form based on its content.

Allow me to elaborate on Himillsy's observa-
tions of Room 207 of the Baxter building. Until
a couple of years ago, it had been part of the
chem lab. Now, State pretended it was an art studio—an aesthetic silk purse that couldn't dis-
guise its sulfuric pigskin lining. Impotent gas jets
poked their chromium heads out of the center of
the five twelve-foot-long tables we used for

desks. The flat, fossilized remains of countless experiments covered their surfaces—a dropcloth of compounds and colors which would have made even Pollock queasy.

At precisely two twenty-five we entered and sat, facing what used to be the blackboard, having given place to a blank cinder-block expanse dotted with a rectangle of holes. The chalk ledge had stayed behind. The door was to the rear left of the room, and it loomed with the vague suggestion that you'd be wise to cast an eye to it now and then. I was at the front table, farthest to the right, Mike to my left, Himillsy and two others to his.

I had decided at the last minute to go with my original idea—the one that Hims had scotched—I would put up a blank piece of paper, say my word was "big," and then say it was so big that only a small section of it was visible. It still seemed not quite right, but I just couldn't think of anything else.

At two twenty-seven, the fluorescent lights snapped on, and what had been a dusky waiting room became a garish operating theater. Sorbeck strode in and sat on a wooden armchair off to the rear right of us, which annoyed me—you could only look to the front or to him, but not both. He removed his pipe from a leather envelope the color of dried ketchup, loaded, and lit. Its invisible custard smoke took a stroll though the room.

"Morning. We'll go one at a time. Put your solution up on the front wall and face the class, please. Let's begin from the first row, left to right, and work our way back. Starting with you."

He nodded to Kirk Brutenhausen. Sophomore, Drawing major. Dirty blond, B-movie looks, and Da Vinci aspirations. Sigma Chi. Only a so-so draftsman—I'd seen his stuff tacked up in the hallway. He could put out a beautiful line, but his shading was all over the place. I'd glance at it in passing and think, "No, Kurt, *chiaroscuro* means *one* light source on the pear, not fourteen." Dottie worshiped him and he let her lick it up—the rooster in the henhouse of Still Life 201.

Thought his shit was toothpaste.

Now he stood in the front of the room in his Greek letter sweatshirt and madras pants, clutching a small piece of pencil-flecked tracing paper. The look on his face implied he was going to get this troublesome little formality over with toot sweet and sit back down.

"Well, I didn't have time to do much," he said, "it being rush week and all—I'm on the committee. But I have a coupla ideas in the works. Frankly, this one sorta threw me for a loop—I mean, it *is* a pretty nutty assignment. Anyway, I've got this part of a sketch of—"

"Get out."

Sorbeck's Voice. God. He made it into a

bucket of ice water dumped on Brutey's head. Kurt acted as if he was hearing things. He was.

"P-pardon?"

"Of this room. Get. Out."

"But I—"

He stood up and took the pipe out of his mouth. "Son." Held it like a grenade he just yanked the pin out of. "This isn't a classroom, it's an arena. And I'd like nothing more than to scour the floor of it with your mirror-kissing lips. But the thing is, we charge admission here. Your ticket is your assignment, completed. Then I rip it in two and may or may not give you back the stub for your scrapbook. No exceptions. Last Thursday I made that as clear as you probably think your skin is."

Jesus Christ.

"Rush on home, Stigma Guy. Rush rush." Then, putting a hand to his ear and his eyes skyward, "I think I hear your committee trying to make a decision without you."

Kurt was a statue of shock. In my mind I could see the mop handle sticking out of his backside. I made it out to be about four inches in diameter, eight or so feet long, and covered with Sorbeck's fingerprints. The floor was now spotless.

Then the teacher cast his net of displeasure out, over us all. "Well, we're off to a flying start here, aren't we, kids?" Fiendish and dark: "Listen up, folks. If there's *ANYONE* else here who mistook this course for the Sigma Chi ice-cream social and does not have his ticket, then rush along with Stiggy right now, while you still have the legs to do it."

No one moved. Except Kurt, of course, dragging his pole, his best "I don't have to take this" look on his face. Rubbery legs betrayed him though, as he fumbled with his books and closed the door behind him.

See ya 'round campus, Kurt.

"I mean it."

I thought: "Sir, there's not a soul in the room that doesn't believe you."

"Next."

Maybelle went to the front. She held her project in her hand and faced the class.

"Whenever you're ready, Miss . . . "

"Maybelle. Maybelle Lee."

"Let's get started, Maybelleen."

"That's Mayb—"

"Are you going to hang your masterpiece on the wall or what?"

Maybelle was gripped with a mild panic, as if the Junior League had just walked through the door and she still couldn't find the dessert forks. "I, I don't have any tape. Y-you didn't tell us to bring any."

"I didn't tell you to wear underwear either, Maybelleen, but I'd put at least fifty down on the chance you've got some keeping your cookies warm right now. Do I win?"

For this, Maybelle had no words.

"You were a guest in this plantation parlor last Thursday, Miss Lee, and surely must have noticed that this fine institution of ours has not yet deigned to bestow upon us the luxury of thumb tacks and a corkboard facade to accessorize our cunning cinder-block vista. Until they so choose, we're all just going to have to make the best of it.

"Would someone be so kind as to supply Miss Maybelleen with some adhesion?"

Mike volunteered, and soon she was standing with white-gloved hands held crisscrossed in front of her sky blue gingham shirtdress, her project suspended to the right, ready and waiting. Her word was "inky."

"Well *well*. What have we here?"

It was hand-done in black (ink, one supposed), a club-fisted attempt at thick, gooey, script—the sort you see on the lid of a box of chocolates that appear to be delicious and taste like wads of dried, brown housepaint.

"I calligraphied it myself. Back at home, this past weekend."

The molten clump of amoebic letters tilted

slightly downward to the right, as if it were falling asleep, and a trail of smudges emerged mysteriously at the middle of the "n," paraded on towards the "k," to the "y," and continued off the crumpled page. The whole thing was about two and a half inches off-center to the right, as if trying to escape. I was rooting for it.

Maybelle: "You could take calligraphy at Miss Cress's. You know, for place cards at supper? People just love to see their names all fancy and fine. The teacher always held mine up to show. It's not a skill for everyone, but I'm just crazy for it. Picked it up right away, like riding a bicycle."

Yeah, off a cliff. Damn the torpedoes, Maybelleen.

"So I thought why not do the word 'calligraphy' in *calligraphy*. I thought that was clever. But then I thought, 'Calligraphy' is really a twenty-five-cent word, isn't it? What if people didn't know what it meant?' I might be leaving someone out of the fun, and that's just not fair. So I changed it to 'ink,' which I didn't think anyone would have any trouble with, and it still seemed to make sense. So I put the paper on my drawing table, picked up my brush and bottle, dipped it in, and you know what? Got it on the first try. Usually it takes three or four, but this one was it, I knew. I started to put the cap back on the bottle, and *then*,"

She paused, to prepare us for some unfathomable catastrophe.

"*Then*, my *cat* jumped up on the table and walked right over it, proud as you please. Well, you can imagine my state. Of course the ink was nothing *like* dry, and he tracked it all over. I grabbed him as soon as I could and wrapped each of his paws with little paper bags and Scotch tape before he could wreck anything else, but the damage was done. I'd have to start over. Then it came to me like a bolt from the blue—eerie, really, one of those coincidences that just gives you the spooks." Another pause. "I suddenly realized that my cat's *name* is *Inky*. Because he's black. So I just took out my brush, and added a 'y' to the end of the word. And I looked at it and I thought, 'Yes, that's good old Inky alright. Can't stand to be away from his mommy, even when she's working.' So I kept it."

Sorbeck waited patiently through all of this. I wondered whether his critique should start at her neck and work its way slowly to her midsection; or just make a horizontal incision across her stomach, remove her large intestine, and place it in her mouth—Capone's preferred method with squealers. Whichever, we were about to find out. I glanced over at Himillsy, who looked like she was watching a really, really good movie.

Sorbeck finally spoke. "So, what was Helen like?"

"Pardon? Helen who?"

"Keller, your calligraphy teacher. Was she any better at embossing?"

She digested this, then tried to make speech. Finally, she managed, "That's, that's—"

"THAT'S the only explanation for the aborted fetus of letterforms that you've stuck to the wall."

Maybelle's eyes became saucers.

"Miss Lee, during your studies at Miss Crass,"

"Miss Cress—"

"Did Miss *Crass*'s calligraphy curriculum, by any chance, include the study of a book entitled *The Universal Penman*, compiled by one George Bickham?"

"N-no. We used . . . the Stratford guide to commercial lettering."

"I see. Maybelleen, I have a special assignment for you, due a week from today."

"Yes?"

He waited for her to do something. She didn't.

"Grab a pencil and paper, my dear, you're not a tape recorder."

Mike obliged her again, and she did her shattered best to copy down the instructions.

"Miss Lee, you are to go to the library. That is the especially large edifice overrun with *books*, located just northwest of the Natatorium. Ask someone for directions. You are to sign out the title I just mentioned. You don't even have to look it up—its Dewey decimal number is Bic 4.093-21. I want you to study it, and, safe with the knowledge that Inky is either heavily sedated or nowhere in the vicinity, replicate page ninety-two. Twenty times. And Maybelleen?"

Her eyes, soggy, rose to his. His tone grew softer, easing up.

"I'm crazy about calligraphy myself. And when you see this book, you'll know why. Your real problem with calligraphy, my dear, is that you've never seen any."

Then he threw her a bone.

"But, your, ahem, thought process, was actually not bad." Louder now, to everybody, "Important lesson here, folks, seriously: Fate gave little Maybelleen the lemons, and she made lemonade. Good for her. Her grade is a vitamin C-plus."

Maybelle didn't walk to her chair, she waded, through a mire of anguish and defeat.

"Shame she had to go and drink it, and turn it into pee. Next."

Himillsy's turn. I thought she might give me a little wish-me-luck glance. Didn't. She sprang up to the wall, mounted her piece, and stepped to its side.

A stark, black leaf of paper. Not a mark on it.

No. It couldn't be. She must have attached the wrong side. She'd notice in a second. I tried to get her attention, no luck. Mills, you usually notice these things immediately.

He took it in, only slightly interested.

"And your word is?"

"Kimprobdagian."

That got him. For a breath, anyway.

"*Excuse* me? What the piss does *that* mean?"

Himillsy, unfazed: "Grandmother Dodd used to use it now and then. Kimprobdag was the name of a city in the Ukraine near the village where she grew up. Oh, the old country, so many memories. Anyway, most of the buildings there were painted black. When she first went as a child, she thought it was the biggest thing she'd ever seen, and after that, whenever she wanted to say that something was *huge,* she'd say it was Kimprobdagian. We'd all just reel. Such a *panic,* the old thing."

No. This wasn't happening.

"She's dead now, gone to her reward," she said, in a more somber tone, wringing it for the sympathy vote.

And you're going to join her right after class, Hims.

"Little girl," started Sorbeck, politely, "I have a question for you."

"Yes?" With the trace of a smile and eyebrows aloft, she tilted her doll's head sideways and became Audrey Hepburn taking questions at a press conference for UNICEF.

"Just how does a girl with such a slight frame, such as yourself—your *sylph*," she nodded to this, now a little worried, "find room for the Kimprobdagian ration of shit you just tried to nourish me with?"

"I—"

"The word, darlin'. Where is it?"

"Oh, that," she said, restored to relief. "Right there," she pointed to the jet rectangle. "At least, part of it anyway. You're only seeing a small detail, probably the middle of the 'K'. Nothing Kimprobdagian would ever fit onto an eleven-by-fourteen inch piece of paper."

Thanks, Hims. I thought I knew what Treachery was, to say nothing of Friendship. Thanks for clearing them *both* up.

"That's actually, darlin', a pretty good idea. Congrats," he said, mildly approving.

Yeah, mine. What was I going to do now? Mike was next, and then me. I *could* just put it up there like a moron and explain that we had the same idea, ha ha, funny world that way . . .

"Except for two things." Then again . . .

"Yes?" said Himillsy, who, accustomed to success in these situations, had already begun to ceremoniously take down the ebony page. She stopped in midgesture.

"Kimprobdag . . . Is that anywhere near Brobdingnag?"

She dropped her arms. Paused. "It—"

"I'm no expert on the Ukraine, gosh knows, but it sure *sounds* a lot like Brobdingnag."

I didn't know what this had to do with anything, but if it made Mills squirm, I was all for it. And right now, she was a gecko on a white-hot parking lot.

"As in where Gulliver goes after Lilliput. As in the land where he is tiny and everyone else huge, which spawned the term 'Brobdingnagian.' As in tremendously large. As in the book by Dean Swift, which is peeking out of your handbag—Penguin Classic, with the orange bands at the top and bottom; and the Gill Sans thirty-six-point title, all caps, centered and medium weight, in black on the white band in the middle. One of the designer Tschichold's prouder moments, when he finally woke the hell up and joined the twentieth century."

Hims kept her composure, I'll give her that.

"Girleen," Sorbeck explained, "we *both* know that the only Kimprobdag is the one you just crapped out of that pretty little cake hole of yours."

Which was now agape.

"You like to fart your little fictions and let everyone get a whiff, I can tell. Your stolen clevernesses. Clever to *you*, anyway. You just *drip* with that daily, dull, nagging ache to get *away* with something. Pulls you out of bed in the morning. No?"

Hims: fist on hip. Livid.

"And you know what? I don't care. Kimprobdag, Brobdingnag, Robbed'ngagged, what's the dif? Swift probably based it on something else too. That's not the problem, and neither is your idea. Your idea is still great. Superb, in fact. Idea: A minus, maybe even an A."

Thank you.

"Execution: F. Do you know why?"

Whether she did or didn't, Mills wasn't about to give him the satisfaction of so much as a peep. No cracks, no sarcasm, no scatological rebound. No jokes. Just mute, broadcast rage.

"Hey, lighten up, Girlygirl. Life is short. The reason is, this solution would be appropriate to *any* word that has to do with immense size and is therefore invalid. It could be Monstrous, Colossal, Gargantuan, Whopper, Titanic, and so on. The point was to be specific. I think that was quite clear. Maybelline's stinky Inky was at least, personally (or cattily, or what have you) referenced to *him*."

Maybelle brightened a little, probably trying

to turn the electric fan of her pulse to a slower speed.

"In fact, none of you should have to explain any of these. I should be able to walk right up to them and get it. For instance, if this was turned into a poster for the travel bureau of Kimprobdag and you walked past it on the street, would you be able to tell what it was? And if you were a wing nut like Girleenie and *did* figure it out, would you be tempted to go there? Would it give you *any* idea of what the place was like?"

Himillsy, not budging.

"On the other hand, at least I have *some* picture of Inky in my mind. Execrably rendered, but there he is: A selfish, thoughtless little bastard who would claw Maybelleen's eyeballs right out of her skull and gulp them down like mouse heads the minute he thought there was nothing else to eat. Like all cats. I should know, I've got two of the little shits myself—all over everything. Madness. Anyway, enough of this for now." He turned to the class. "You all, I'm sure, have digested the idea and wouldn't dream of replicating the little girl's folly. And darlin' . . . ," Sorbeck looked at Hims with an executioner's mirth, "never let your mouth write a check that your ass can't cash." He let her face explode and put itself back together, then, "Onward! Park yourself, Girlygirl, tempus fugit. Next."

Hims ripped the paper like a giant Band-Aid from the wall and stomped her tiny black patent leather feet to the table. She still wouldn't look at me.

Mike went to the front and carefully attached his work. It was my turn after his. What, what, *what* was I going to do? My mind raced to out-speed the impending doom and took stock of my resources: my tote of pens and brushes, my Geo Sci textbook, my notebook, and my pad of D'Rathope watercolor paper. Not much to work with . . .

"Alright, let's see what we got." I looked up.

Mike stood next to his solution: the word "HOT." He had made the letters out of match-sticks. But the term "made" wasn't adequate—he'd *sculpted* clusters of matches into a real typeface. His hours in the Belly were well spent. I was right—he was going to ace all of us. The craftsmanship was impeccable, as if 'HOT' wasn't an adjective, but a cozy country inn that had this sign hanging out front. The raised, rounded letterforms almost filled the allotted space and gleamed under the lights—he must have varnished it. My heart sank, it was so beautiful. Now, no matter what I did, it would look pathetic by comparison. Jesus, I had to think, *think* . . .

"Son, what is your word?"

The question caught Mike (and everyone else) off guard. It was quite obvious what his word was—what the hell did Sorbeck think? If he wanted to embarrass the guy, he was overdoing it. Anyone could get a blush out of Mike just by looking at him.

And why bother, anyway? His piece was great, and he'd obviously spent a lot of time on it. Sorbeck should have been quite pleased.

But then, this was before any of us knew him at all.

"H-hot?"

"I see. Would you extend your right index finger for me please?"

He did, as if he was about to be sworn under oath.

"Well done. Now, would you take your finger and place it on one of the letters? I'll let you choose which one." I was starting to get it, but Mike still stared out from the prison of his fear. Sorbeck repeated the question with growing irritation. Mike's hand slowly moved and hovered over the "H." Then,

"TOUCH IT!" The tremulous finger alit softly onto the slivers of sculpted wood as if they were forbidden flesh, and the Commander was pleased. Calm, he said, "Okay now. Keep it there for a moment while I ask you a question." Mike nodded his head and waited. "Now, I want you to think quite hard about this, don't rush the answer, work it through." Mike was paralyzed. Sorbeck made the wind-up:

"Son, your finger. The one on the letter?" A pause, then the pitch:

"You got a blister on it yet?" Steeerike one.

"No, sir." Steeerike two. Mike, dumb as a truck.

"Well then, it's not very *hot,* is it?"

"Uh. No." And three.

"So, given the assignment, we'd have to say you get an F then, wouldn't we?"

"I . . . " His face was falling, slowly, like a punctured zeppelin " . . . guess so." He lowered his finger.

"Would you like to get an A?"

Mike looked up at him, awakened from a miserable dream. Sorbeck pulled something out of his pocket and tossed it his way. "Heads up."

It landed into his cupped hands with a heavy click. I didn't have to see it to guess what it was. Mike's eyes confirmed it with blanched mortification.

"A or F, m'boy, up to you."

Mike fumbled and managed to form a word:

"Bestine . . ."

"Pardon?"

"Bestine. I used Bes*tine . . .*"

Oh. Oh no.

"Bestine," Sorbeck crooned, to the tune of "Tangerine." *"Bestine, I burn for you . . ."*

"But—"

"We don't have forever. Choose. A or F. Five . . ."

Confused? Allow me: Bestine is a brand of rubber cement thinner. Mike had used it—quite a bit, to put the matches together.

"Four . . ."

It comes in heavy, metal utility cans. Like gasoline. Only the difference between it and gasoline is . . .

"Three . . ."

Gasoline isn't nearly as flammable.

"Two . . ." Not by a long shot. Mike somehow made himself flip open the top of the Zippo lighter and flick the flint at the bottom of the page, to his work—his hours and days of painstaking work. The device merely sparked.

"O—"

Which was enough. The wall burst apart before his cowering figure, opening a small window into hell. It sounded as if someone had unfurled a huge blanket in a high wind, and the glare eclipsed the fluorescent lights into nothing. I felt a puff of searing breath on my cheeks and wondered if Mike would ever have eyebrows again. Maybelle let loose with a small, popping shriek. Almost as quickly as it had come, the blaze was gone, leaving a dark poster-sized patch on the cinder-block wall—reduced to, well, cinders. Sorbeck's face held mild interest.

"Gee, when it was going, it was an A."

Mike trudged back to his seat and set the Zippo on the table. A virus of dread overtook me.

"But that didn't last too long, did it?" The teacher picked up the lighter and relit his pipe. "You see, Bestine, the key to this assignment is choosing the right word. *Then* you go on with the proper execution. If you'd just gone for 'Volatile,' we wouldn't have had to go that extra step. Does everyone see what I mean?"

Hmm. Yes.

I took the pad of paper out of my satchel. It was (bless you D'Rathope), eleven by fourteen. I removed a sheet and scanned it. D'Rathope is very good paper, probably the best—each piece has a little something extra the company puts there. I found what I was looking for on the page and ripped a small corner out of it.

"Next." Here we go. Christ. I scribbled something on a piece of scrap paper and tossed it in front of Himillsy. I glared at her until she picked it up—it was the least she could do.

I went to the front of the room, which still reeked from the smoldering remains of Mike's little armageddon. I glanced over at his drained, defeated phiz, and tried to ignore it, taping the

piece of blank paper to the charred wall, vertically, with the small tear in the upper left-hand
corner. For a moment I was struck by the con-
trast of the pristine sheet against the murky ruin
of the wall. But then I turned and stood next to
it. My living daylights had long since fled. He
dove right in.

"Don't tell me. It's Kimprobdag on a snowy
day."

I took a breath. "Not at all, sir."

"Boy, this better be good."

I tried to keep my trembling in check, "Look .
. . harder."

"You know, if the word is 'invisible', you flunk.
Too obvious."

"It's not."

A mixture of anger and boredom. "Right.
Look, it's the same as girleeny's—could be anything, whatever you say it is. Nice try. You fail."

Say it. Make myself say it. Powerless.

"Sit down, son."

"Mr. Sorbeck . . . "

"Winter."

Winter? Brrr. "Winter," going for broke, my
tissue of confidence soaked, disintegrating. "I
selected and wrote down my word . . . on Monday. She has it, in her hand." I nodded towards
Himillsy. She straightened, and held up the
piece of paper I gave her above the table, on cue

as if we'd practiced it. Winter Sorbeck now started to like this, I could tell, though he pretended to hate it.

"Okay, liddlegirl," he crooned like W. C. Fields, only more frightening, "What's the good word? Enlighten us all."

Mills opened the piece of paper, gave her throat a squeak:

"Hope."

Every sheet of D'Rathope paper has a small, embossed water mark of the company's name on it. All I did was remove the corner with the "D'Rat," and left the rest.

Sorbeck: Iron-faced. Livid. Quiet. "Give me that." He extended his arm and made Hims come up and pass it to him. He looked at it, and at me. Then, never taking his eyes from mine, face vacant as my attempt, held it up in his left hand, crushed it, and let it fall to the ground.

"Gee. You're just a happy guy then, aren't ya?" He aped hammy despair, like a cast member from *Lifeboat*: *"There is. No hope."*

Oh, well, I tried. Next major, please. This one's too weird. I said, "No, it's there, really. Just look for it." He came wearily towards the front of the room. Halfway there he saw it. He knew. "It's small and barely exists; it's high above the void, but it's there . . ." I began to remove the paper from the wall. Jeez, who was I fooling—how corny could I get? I tried something else, in franker tones. "Actually, a blank piece of paper always says 'hope' to me, until someone goes and screws it all up . . . "

"Tell ya what, Happy. Surprise. Now *that* I buy."

The blood left my head. He was Jekyll again. Unnerving.

"Kiddies, let me tell you what just happened. Happy here forgot to bring his project. Which, I noticed, he only discovered shortly before Bestine's went up like a three-dollar dress on a two-dollar whore (Sorry, Maybelleen). This scared the poop out of him. But instead of giving me excuses, he made a plan. Not a great one, but doable in the time he had—about two minutes. He even had to rely on the little girl from Robbed'ngagged here, who's a wing nut to begin with, to deliver at the last second and make it seem worked out way in advance. When challenged on its flimsy quality, he didn't give up. He explained why he did what he did, though I wish he had held in there a little longer.

"This is known, kidlings (allow me the cliché), as thinking on your feet, which none of you will ever be lucky enough to escape having to do. Remember that. Hap, I was waiting for a much better payoff than 'hope.' Jeez. Maybe something a little more appropriate like 'brains.'

But it's only the second week. Think what geniuses you'll all be by June." He made his way closer to the wall, leaned in, and squinted at the damage.

"I must say though," genuinely now, to no one or himself, "that I loved the image of the untouched paper in the middle of the scorch mark." The reverie broke and he turned to me. "Hap, if you would have said, 'This is Switzerland during World War Two', all would have been forgiven. You'd have gotten at least a B plus. But you didn't. Was a great image though. I think I'll steal it for something that I'm working on.

"That's another thing—listen up, folks, cardinal rule: *Never* show me anything that you don't want me to steal."

Or Himillsy.

"Okay, kiddies, I've run out of steam. Everyone else, you all get Cs. Nobody gives a shit about grades anyway. If you don't believe me, wait till you're forty and the only grade you'll care about is the angle of your driveway. Now, next class is the first typography lesson. We'll be starting with Bodoni. Read up on it in the Tschichold and try not to get too distracted by what an asshole he is. Just concentrate on the form of the typeface and its history. I want you all to find and bring into class three examples of its use. See you Thursday."

We groggily started to move, not quite sure we were allowed to. My shirt pits sopping. Even Himillsy's brow was moist.

"But Hap."

Everyone stopped and looked at me. Winter was calm but dead serious.

"You will remember to bring your work to class. And if you ever try that again." He shouldered his coat and turned, walking out of the room, already starting to forget me.

"I'll make today seem like a *lot* of fun."

• • •

We staggered into the hallway, slow with relief. Hims looked at her watch. "Well, that *was* a hoot. Sort of like the McCarthy hearings, only without the laughs." She opened her bag. "Thanks for all the advance notice on your little plan. Next time you want to saw me in half, try putting me in a box first, Mandrake."

"And NEXT time you steal one of my ideas, remind me to KILL you first!" I said the words "next" and "kill" way too loudly. Screaming. She pivoted. It was more of a release than anything else—I was immediately sorry.

"I didn't *steal* it!" Her eyes met mine for a brief standoff, then darted back to her purse. "You left that idea squealing on my doorstep!"

She took out her compact and started to retouch her warpaint. "I just took it in and gave it a teat to draw from—improved on it *immensely*, ha ha." Eyes to the sky. "For all the good it did. Christ, I'm melting. *Dying* for a beer. Let's beat it."

"Where's Maybelle, is she alright?"

"She's in the can, wringing out her face. C'mon, pull your oar, before she tries to climb into our lifeboat." She was off. I trailed after her, helpless to do anything else. Was there ever any choice but to follow? After all, the lifeboat was *ours* . . .

· · ·

"I should have called him on it." Himillsy took a drag on her first cigarette of the day. We were waiting for beers in the Skeller—our bombed shelter.

"On what?" I was letting my anger evaporate, still dizzy from the events of the class, the base-ball-sized hailstorm of ideas. Hims pondered something far away and then came back to Earth.

"He was wrong about Maybelle's—it was true to the concept of 'inky.'" She drew in the smoke, let it go. "So *what* if her first choice was 'callig-raphy.' She ended up with 'inky,' and that's what mattered. Her presentation was blotchy, goopy, and smeared. If that's not inky what is, for

Chrissake." Took another puff and put it out.
"Regardless of her mongoloid cat. He played us
all for fools." Meaning Sorbeck.

"He knew his audience." I said, not caring
about the ramifications. Odd for her to defend,
of all people, Maybelle—but it wasn't a defense
of *her* so much as an attack on Winter. "Some of
us are barn-sized targets, aren't we?" I asked.

"Not anymore. Happy."

"What? You're *dropping*?"

Hims looked at me as if I were nuts. "You
want to go through *that* twice a week for the rest
of the semester? Please." She signaled for Greck.

"Well, isn't that a little hasty? I mean, yeah,
he's a bit odd, but you've got to admit," I wasn't
sure where I was going with this, "He's. It's.
Interesting, isn't it?"

"So was Hiroshima. At a *distance.*"

That made me angry. "What are you scared
of?" She didn't like the question. I didn't go on,
but I could have. I could have said "Are you suddenly so afraid of being challenged by someone
other than Garnett? Of finding a teacher who, for
the first time in your life, might actually be
smarter than you are, than Garnett is? Who might
actually, God forbid, *teach* you something?"

Winter was a scary guy, yes. But wasn't he
exactly what we'd been waiting for? The fact that
he was even here at State was miraculous in

itself. She had to know that. I said, "Look. Why not give it another shot. He's not going to do a critique every class, or even every week, and you know he just wants to rattle us. Besides, he obviously likes you." This had an effect on her, which she (poorly) tried to hide.

"Sorry," she demurred, "I scratched necrophilia off my list a long time ago."

· · ·

As it turned out I didn't even have to coax her to stick with Art 127—the Burser did it for me—wouldn't let her out. We were too far into the semester—everything else for the period was filled, it was too late to declare an audit; and, sealing it: she'd dropped too many times in the past. For once the bureaucracy of the hive worked in my favor.

At the next class we went over the typographic samples we'd collected, passing them up to Winter for discussion. When he wasn't in full critique-battle mode, he was much easier to deal with.

"You," he nodded to someone in the back of the room, "wutcha got."

A tow-headed boy in a black turtleneck and black work pants stood up. Mummy thin. He took a crumpled piece of paper out of his pocket.

Instead of passing it forward he began to recite, with tortured, monotone gravity,

"If the clouds could speak, they would hate you. If—"

"If I had a gun I'd stab you. What the hell is *that*?"

"It's a poem." The boy's eyes were hollow and glazed. "I wrote it last night."

"With what, the hand that wasn't holding the needle? It's crap." Sorbeck rapped his pipe on the table to empty it, sending a spray of moist ashes to the floor. He did that a lot, and it never failed to fill me with awed repulsion. "Besides, the two actions are mutually exclusive. You don't need to be able to speak in order to hate someone! Don't you think there are legions of loathing mutes out there?" Winter paused, amazed and horrified that he'd even been brought to ask such a question. "Jesus, why am I *bothering* with this? Read Whitman, for Chrissakes. Mr . . ."

"David."

"David what."

"David. David David."

"David David?"

"Yes."

"Let me guess, your parents were twins."

"No. I've released myself from the tyranny of a bourgeois societal abattoir that brands its cow-like subjects with meaningless labels in order to more efficiently herd them." He was serious. Winter threw it right back at him.

"No, you've forsaken your family's good name in a sadly misguided exchange for a false identity even more dull and conformist than the one you think you're escaping. At some point you will grow up, and the very notion of it will make you wince in your sleep."

David David stood unblinking, impervious. He probably heard it all the time. *Lived* for it.

"Plant it, D Squared. Bestine?" Mike handed in another hand-rendering of the word "Hot," but in red and set in the typeface we were assigned.

"Bestine, give it up. You're smitten with this idea and it's making a fool of you. Type is nice though. Everyone?" He stood. "*Never* fall in love with an idea. They're whores: if the one you're with isn't doing the job, there's always, always, *always* another."

• • •

Two days later, we were on our way to the Hutzle Union building to renew Mills's campus parking sticker when suddenly she chirped, "Hey! It's the Happy-Clappies! Let's go give 'em a spark."

As you've no doubt deduced by now, Miss Dodd had a rather thorny view of religion, which was best summed up by the fact that she got thrown out of vacation Bible school at age eleven for making a St. Sebastian toothpick holder in Crafts.

Every now and then, walking past Old Main, one would spot the Campus Crusaders, a flock of prematurely Redeemed Souls who felt it wasn't enough that God was your Creator, he also had to be your Pal.

"Look at them. It's *illegal* to be that happy."

A chunky girl in a red plaid skirt who *appeared* to be completely normal casually walked up to Himillsy and asked, just a little too loudly, "Did you know that Jesus loves you?" She handed us a pamphlet with a cartoon drawing on the front of the crucified Savior, bleeding like new dungarees in the wash. He looked ecstatic, as if he'd just won the Lottery. Hims took it and used it to fan herself, even though it was just below freezing.

"Of course, dear, and we're just dying to get married, but Mummy is dead set against it." Hims leaned into her, very conspiratorial, "He's N.O.K.D., and if we elope she'll cut us off."

Our little Merry Magdalene didn't seem to understand. She turned to me, on to her next mission, and said, now a tad unsure of herself, "God loves you too."

"Obviously," I said. "I'm white, I have a penis, and fabulous taste."

Himillsy's surprise had just the right note of

archness. "Darling! A penis? Really! Why didn't you tell me? Whose is it?"

"Not sure. I haven't opened it yet."

"Oh come, let's do!" she said, taking my arm. "You must really rate! All *I* got was a slash that smells like carp and leaks blood every month!" She winked at the girl—whose face was as blank as her checks to the Church.

We skipped away, arm in arm. Hims looked back to the group, right before we made the corner, and shouted, "*Praise* Him!"

• • •

The problem for the next formal critique was, thankfully, less opaque than the first. You had to design a symbol, or "trademark" for yourself, and apply it to an eight-and-a-half-by-eleven piece of stationery. The only hitch was you couldn't use any typography. You had to hand it in anonymously, and if he couldn't figure out which one was yours, you failed.

I did *not* care to exchange ideas on this one with Hims, thank you very much.

Instead I sat in the Belly that night and toured the brothel of my head for the right approach to show me some leg, as per Winter's quaint comparison. I wondered if my Social Security number would count as typography. Probably.

Next—symbols, markings, identification. A way of saying, "This is me!" without words. A photo of myself? Cop-out. A drawing? I turned a piece of black conte crayon end over end in my fingers. Thinkthinkthink.

In the high school library, during study halls when I found an especially brilliant or idiotic passage in a book, I'd make a comics word balloon around it, pointing to the margin. Then in the space I'd draw a cartoon of my head, a Disney version, saying it—marking a trail to nowhere for some poor shmo after I was long gone. Hmmm. I picked up a piece of D'Rathope (I was now a lifetime customer). Whoops. Smudged it. Rats. Wiped my fing—

Wait.

My pal, the Almighty, had already *given* me a trademark—*ten* of them. I took out my ink pad, flipped up the lid. Carefully pressed my left thumb onto it, and then rolled it onto the paper, like they do on *Dragnet*.

A perfect oval.

I drew a neck and shoulders underneath it, in a dress shirt, jacket, and tie. Coup d'état: gave it glasses like mine.

Liked it.

Didn't dare *love* it . . .

• • •

BASIC INTERLUDE (11)

The problem with Top to Bottom is that it's unAmerican. Ellis Island, the Conestoga Trail, Horatio Alger, and all that. We want to begin in the depths and climb our way upward. But our typographic system argues against this and wins, and images follow suit. So we not only know that the enemy is coming in from the left, he is also landing at the top and working his way downward.

Blame it, as with all things mortal, on gravity. In the end—for better, for worse, it's only natural—what goes up, must etc., etc.

So then, are we forever compelled to put our most important information at the top? Certainly, certainly not. Such thinking, everyone, is not what these Little Lessons are meant to induce. They are the Weather Conditions, not Rainmaking.

Let's say that on our surface, we want to convey a sense of . . . alienation? Perhaps we're doing a poster for a Beckett play. Rockaby, say. You'd be well suited to have nothing at the top at all (read it, you'll see what I mean). Rather, it would be more appropriate to have the enemy's eye land in a void (black, probably, but that's up to you—what does the set look like?) and dog-paddle for a while, before letting itself give up and sink to the bottom, where it finally lands on the title, the theater, the address, the curtain time.

And from there, to nothing.

THE SECOND CRITIQUE.

Art 127 (Introduction to Graphic Design),
Winter Sorbeck, instr.

For which we are asked to design a personal identity
mark, or "logo," for use as a symbol to be placed on
business cards and the like in order to invite inquiry,
generate capital, etc. No typographic information, of
any kind, may be used.

"Okay, pass them up."

We handed our papers forward. Without looking, he put them in his briefcase and snapped it shut. "Fine. Now, can anyone tell me what that assignment was *about*?" Silence. He sighed. "Nobody?"

Nobody.

"Thought so. Surprise, kiddies—pop quiz."

Pop quiz? In art class?

He pointed to a box of Magic Markers and a stack of poster board. "Everybody will take one of each, please." Once we had done it and returned to our seats, he spoke, pacing across the front.

"Alright, so here's the rub: It's February. You're stuck in the middle of nowhere, on the side of the road. All you have is the clothes on your back, a Magic Marker, and a big ol' piece of paper. Now," he grinned. "Get home."

Mike raised his hand.

Winter nodded. "Bestine."

"How much time do we have?"

"Good question. I'm very glad you asked that, Besty," he said. "In fact, nobody do anything yet. I just want you to think about it. Five minutes, then do a rough sketch of your solution on a piece of scrap paper." He left the room. I could hear his muffled voice, talking to someone on the pay phone in the hallway.

We sat.

I formed a couple of ideas in my head (howdy, girls!), picked one, and worked it out. Winter broke the silence.

"Okay everyone. Field trip. Grab your gear." He pulled on a bulky navy pea coat, black felt mariner's hat, and tan leather gloves. "And don't forget the markers and boards."

A university bus was waiting in front of the building. Soon we were leaving the campus limits. Hims slumped next to me, silent. Maybelle and Mike ended up together, in the seat across from us. Mabes and Bestine: the stoppable force and the movable pole. We headed north, towards Blue Mountain. The sky was coconut ice cream. Flat, fallow fields, under mattress-thick snow, stretched east and west to the horizon. After about ten minutes, a small stand of fir trees appeared to the left, and we slowed to a stop. Winter stood. "Heads up, kidlings. Everybody off." We grudgingly followed him out. Air felt like ten degrees, if that.

"Thank goodness I brought my ear muffs," muttered Maybelle.

"Listen up!" Winter shouted through the wind. "Here's how it'll work. The class will hide behind those trees, out of sight of the traffic. One at a time, you will stand at the side of the road, with your sign. A car comes by, you get picked up, it's an A. It keeps going, you drop one letter grade. Second picks you up, it's a B. Third, it's a C. Four cars and no luck, you fail. Let's move it out." We crossed the road, headed for the trees, waited.

Winter leaned into the vehicle's window, said something to the driver, and pulled out his brief-case, coming to join us.

Then the bus made a three-point turn and drove away.

"Hey!" Mabes screamed. Winter smiled.

"Can't have a back door, sweetheart. Might be tempted to use it." It shrank in the distance. Ohmigod, it was really leaving. "Now, aren't you all glad I didn't let you commit your little thoughts to the boards already? Show of hands, how many of you are going to ditch your original idea? C'mon, don't be shy, it won't affect your grade." Just about all of us raised our mitts. I flirted with the impulse to run, to escape. To where? No. He was our key to get out of this. "Thought so. You're thinking about it differently now, aren't you? I'll bet that back there, in our semiheated little classroom, you were trying to figure out how to make it pretty. But right now, Graphic Design doesn't have to be pretty. Graphic Design just has to save you from getting frostbite."

The site proved well chosen, because as desolate as it was, the road had a fairly steady stream of cars, shuttling people between campus and the Blue Mountain ski resort. There was actually one within sight about every five minutes or so.

"Okay, who's first?"

"ME, thank you," said Himillsy, bolting to the roadside, more than ready to extricate herself from this ridiculous plight.

She stood on the shoulder and scrawled something on the board. Then she threw off her floor-length hooded cream woolen cape. As luck would have it, she was wearing one of her own Hello! dresses—a full-skirted sleeveless number made of a cotton so red that in this light it fried your eyeballs. Practically a stop sign.

"She'll freeze to death!"

"Don't bet on it, Maybelleen."

Then she lifted her sign, horizontal, up to her mouth and clenched it in her teeth. Hands behind her back, Hims made herself into the top half of her head, a sign, and a laser-red skirt. She had written:

I AM
NOT
ARMED

In about thirty seconds, a blue Ford station wagon approached, coming from town, on the opposite side. She pointed herself in its direction. The car spun in a wild U-turn and sidled up to her. Mills tossed her sign and ran up to the driver—a kind-looking middle-aged fat man. They exchanged about three words, and she got into the backseat. He put it in neutral, opened the door, went to the roadside, collected her things, and placed them on the passenger seat in front.

She rolled down her window, waved in our direction like the Queen on Coronation Day, and they were off. Winter clicked his tongue and shook his head.

"I just hope she leaves enough of the poor bastard intact so his family can perform a decent burial." He sighed. "Next!"

"Me, please? I'm FREEZING." Mabes was hopping up and down. He nodded.

As could be expected, her approach was a little more conservative than Himillsy's, but it was still pretty clever. She raised it high over her head and knitted her brow.

S.O.S!
SORORITY
PRANK!

"She's weathered her share of those, actually," I offered.

"Not a bad idea," allowed Winter, "though fat lot of good it would do her anywhere else." Soon a van full of the girl's downhill slalom team showed up and took her in.

One by one, people gave it a go. A few got it on the first try, most on second, some the third. No one failed, probably because of our Siberian location and the provincial tenor of the area. It eventually came down to David David, Mike, and me.

"Give it a shot, D Squared."

David D mustered as much energy as he could bear, and shuffled up to the road. There was a weary, pained look on his face, and his sign drooped listlessly at his side. At the sound of an approaching motor, he managed to raise it waist high. It read:

DON'T
EVEN
BOTHER.

"Interesting, but risky," Winter clucked. "Nihilism and Solicitation are uneasy bedfellows."

And indeed, the first car zoomed right on by. But the second driver was intrigued enough to stop. Turns out he was, of all things, a priest.

"Lucky," said Sorbeck, "Probably would have stopped for anybody." He paused. " . . . in theory. God, can you imagine what *they're* going to talk about? Alright, let's finish this up."

Mike looked at me.

"I'd like to go last, actually," I said.

"Okay."

He shook as he walked, either from nerves or the cold, or both. He was Baby June, shoved out onto stage for the first time, looking as if he'd just drunk Drano on a bet. He held his sign to the skies.

PLEASE!
FOR GOD'S
SAKE!!
HELP ME!!

Winter moaned. "Christ, *that's* not going to work."

One, two, three cars whizzed by.

"See? They all think he's on the lam from the laughing academy. I wouldn't go *near* him. Thing is, you don't just design the sign, you've got to consider the whole package—what you're wearing, the look on your face." I felt privileged, as if I were being let in on the secret. "That's why girleeny's really hit the spot."

As the fourth car, an old black DeSoto, approached, Mike abandoned himself to panic and ran into its path. It swerved and laid on the horn.

I was shocked. "Whoa!"

At least he stopped it without injury, running to the driver's window—an old woman who could barely see over the steering column. He beseeched her in pleading tones. She finally acquiesced and let him get in.

"Bestine is *not* the sharpest knife in the drawer." Winter rubbed his eyes, as the buzzing lump was lost to the horizon. "Son, you're on."

Son. I let the idea live in my head for a single, dreamy instant, and filed it away.

I walked to the road.

Scary—the epiphany: I had never, ever been *really* stranded before.

My first idea, right after the bus pulled out, was:

MY TEACHER
IS INSANE.
YOUR ASSISTANCE
APPRECIATED.

But I soon realized this was more a reflection of my mental state than any sort of effective enticement. So I took a cue from David David's, and adjusted it to allow for a broader, hopefully voraciously curious automotive audience:

ASK ME
WHY
I'M HERE!

It took a little longer than the others for a car to show up. Then I heard it. An engine in the distance. I strained to see . . . a green . . . sedan . . . Chevy come into view. A pair of skis strapped to the top. Terrifying. "Please," I thought, "whoever you are, be curious and accepting." Closer, closer. Oh. Merciful God, it slowed down.

And stopped.

The driver, a youngish guy in a Bean checked sweater, rolled down his window.

"Pardon me," I was obscenely polite, clearly uninsane, "but could you possibly give me a ride to North Halls?" He sized me up and said, "Goin' to Pollock."

Close enough. "Thanks! That's great! Um, excuse me a sec, please. Be right back." I ran back to Winter. We'd been there a good two hours. Ears ready to fall off. Just starting to get dark.

"Not bad."

"Oh, thanks." I asked, hopefully: "Aren't you coming with?"

He smirked. "No, Hap. Fair and square."

I was going to insist, but thought better of it.

"See you Thursday," he said.

"Right."

I scooted to the car and popped in.

"So," the guy asked, gunning the engine, "what gives?" As we pulled away I looked out the rear window, at the flowing road, until I was pretty sure I saw a dark shape emerge along the right bank, far away, lost to the twilight. God, is *that* where we were? What a triumph, to get out of nowhere.

Good luck, Dad.

"Well," I turned and looked ahead, towards campus and a hot shower, trying to feel my feet again. "I'm taking this *class* . . ."

• • •

". . . so you see, that's what a logo, for yourself or anyone else, has to do. It has to flag people down, either by invitation or mystery, or any other means, actually." It was two days later. Winter emptied his pipe. *Spack!* "And by limiting your materials I gave you a huge break—one that you can give your*self* anytime you want. Always remember: Limits are possibilities. That sounds like Orwell, I know. It's not—it's Patton. Formal restrictions, contrary to what you might think, free you up by allowing you to concentrate on purer ideas.

"As graphic designers, you want the world as your palette. But beware: You can be crippled by too many choices, especially if you don't know what your goals are. The Hitchhiking Model is a perfect example of how to avoid this, because the parameters are so clear, so black and white. However, few actual graphic design problems are, and it will be up to you to set up rules for yourself in order to properly solve them.

"Had I given each of you an arsenal of squeaky pens spanning the spectrum, I'm sure at least two or three kiddies would still be out there, turned into a popsicle trying to decide between light green and dark green."

• • •

It was almost time for midterms, and Himillsy wanted cram company. We shanghaied a corner booth at Zingorelli's from four P.M. till closing. In order to avoid being kneecapped we'd order a medium Pompeii Pie, and once the cheese had congealed on the leftover crusts, call for another. Mills had taken another fourth-level Art History—Cathedrals—and was deeply regretting it. "I don't know my apse from a holy wall." Flipping madly through texts, notes. "Let's see, early Renaissance churches . . ."

I had Abnormal Psych and Geo Sci to worry about—Nuts and Sluts and Rocks for Jocks.

Over the first two hours at Zingo's, I became aware that Mills was taking a lot of notes. Wasn't it a little late for that? Then I realized she wasn't writing them on paper.

"What are you doing?"

"My most brilliant creation. The Dodd Cheat 'n' Chew." A set of architect's mechanical pens lay open in front of her, next to a box of pencils and her textbooks. She held up her pen. "Ever use one of these? A Ko-inhor .000. Works the best, as long as you keep it going or keep it wet. Tip clogs instantly—Garnett would kill me." It looked like the shortest, thinnest syringe I'd ever seen. "You could do a tat on a tick's tit with one of *these* babies." She licked it, and went back to writing—or copying, more specifically—from her textbooks onto . . . the side of a standard garden variety No. 2 pencil. "Now, Chartres was built in . . ."

"Wow. Can I see one of those?"

She put it back on her tongue, and handed me a finished Dodd Cheat 'n' Chew pencil labeled "Rheims." "Yeth, ut ee carehul. I ha-hent thpray ih ith hix yeh." I took it, gingerly, by the eraser.

"What?"

She went back to writing.

"I said be careful. I haven't sprayed it with fix yet. It gets wet, it's ruined. Water-based ink doesn't clog as fast."

From about two feet away, it looked completely normal. A little darker yellow than usual, but not enough to raise any suspicion. Most of the midterms and finals for the nonelective classes took place in good-sized amphitheaters that held at least three hundred kids. Monitors—grad students, usually—patrolled the aisles to keep everyone honest. But certainly a dutiful test-taker contemplating his or her pencil every now and then wouldn't be the slightest bit out of place.

Ingenious.

"Wow. You must have a surgeon's hand." Those Ripley's Believe-It-Or-Not people who paint *The Last Supper* and *The Battle of Bunker*

Hill onto grains of rice had nothing on her. Encyclopedic amounts of microscopic information, lengthwise, covered each side.

"Actually helps to have a few belts first, but the lighting in the Skeller is abysmal. Guido here practically has search beams on the ceiling."

"And right now he's throwing us dirty looks. Better order another Spitzollini, we don't want our fingernails yanked out."

Midnight. Time to quit. "Whew! I'm beat. I'm never going to get all this down. Just too damn many terms." Was regression a displacement of externalization? Did Approach-Avoidance Conflict generate Cognitive Disorder, or Suprathreshold?

"Want me to make a couple for you?" She waved a drying DCC.

"Wow, would you?"

"Sure. When's the test?"

"Friday."

"No sweat. I'll do 'em tomorrow night. Give me your notes . . . "

• • •

On Friday at ten, she showed up with an envelope, at the door to Piper Pavilion.

"Here ya go. Gotta run. Break a leg."
"Listen, thanks. I really—"
But she was already making tracks.

Felt sort of dirty. Tests were sacred—I'd never so much as ever looked over at my neighbor's outfit, much less their test answers. I told myself I'd only use them as a last resort. At first I was fine, but then:

11.) The Law of Contiguity asserts that:

    A. the distinction between classical and operant conditioning is often hard to make.

    B. is generally considered of little importance in most learning situations.

    C. events experienced together become associated with each other.

    D. maximum conditioning occurs when the CS and UCS are presented at least one minute apart.

Yipes. Could *not* remember. Nuts. I discreetly broke the point on my pencil and pulled a DCC from the envelope. I read, turning it, line for line:

Maybelleen
and Baby Laveen
lay upon the bed.
She spreads them wide,
her buttock and thigh,
and devours his monstrous head.

That was all it said?
    That was all *any* of them said.

    Dodd, you're dead.

· · ·

    "Must you *shriek*?"
    "I am *not* shrieking! In fact, I think I'm being re*mark*ably CALM."
    "Oh, don't be such a sorehead. It was just a *gag*. Besides, I was *going* to do them, really. Ran out of time." Sunday brunch at the Diner. A half-eaten waffle in the shape of the school mascot lay in front of her, in a puddle of cold syrup. Hims was on her third cup of joe. She was so hungover, my head hurt just looking at her.

Didn't make me any less steamed, though. "A gag? I'll be lucky to get anything above an eighty!"

"A schoolie like you? That's rich. *You'd* get extra credit from a loan shark. And I told you, pipe down—I've got a hangover I could sell to *science.*"

"You can't just assume that!"

"Shhh! You could have sized them up ahead of time, Mr. Moto."

"Well, I think I'll just let the dean do that."

She was a little worried now. Good. "And what is *that* supposed to mean?"

Me: very, very serious. "It means *you* have to learn that actions have consequences, and if you're going to put me on the spot, I won't go quietly. Or alone."

She opened her eyes, fully, for the first time that day.

"It also means, that I've composed, addressed, and posted a long, detailed letter to Dean Kane concerning the Dodd Cheat 'n' Chew. Complete with an illuminating profile of the company founder. You can expect to hear from him shortly, I'd guess. Kept a copy, for my files." I pulled out the envelope from my breast pocket and held it chin level.

Her face: White as the paunchy members of the Tuft Trees County Club.

"You. Wouldn't."

I began to put it back in my pocket.

"Let me see that!"

"Don't think so. It's all between the dean and my conscience, now."

She shot across the table and snatched it, knocking over the orange juice and dragging her sweater sleeve through the syrup. People began to stare.

"How *could* you?" Hands shaking, she unfolded it.

> *Himillsy Dodd*
> *defied her God.*
> *And He got even,*
> *while she got odd.*

"April fool." And it *was* too.

There was that wonderful moment when terror alchemized into relief, then tickled fury.

"You *prick!*" Color rushed back into her face.

I was actually thrilled to have her refer to me that way, in that manner—it was permission to scold her, to sweep us into an emotional exchange: "You are lucky I didn't, Miss Molecule. I sure as hell wanted to." I smiled, in spite of myself. Damn, I just could *not* stay mad at her. "You couldn't even come up with more than *one* poem?"

"I *know*, sorry." Hand on heart, trying to slow it down. "My muse just went on *hols* . . ."

• • •

It's hard to pinpoint exactly when The Difference began, but as I bought my ticket from the Beaver Bus Travel Company to go home for Easter, I was really, *really* bothered by the fact that the color and shape of the logo on it (a Chicklet-toothed, dirt brown rodent in a baseball cap, madly waving good-bye with his right hand) did *not* match those on the sign above the sales booth (dark blue and waving with the left). Which was also completely different from the little bastards painted on the sides of the buses AND stamped on the schedule pamphlets (badly printed on a flimsy paper stock completely ill-suited for the wear and tear of the long-term use they were no doubt intended for). And that's when I realized things like this had been occurring to me a lot lately. All signage—indeed, any typesetting, color schemes, and printed materials my eyes pounced on were automatically dissected and held to Draconian standards of graphic worthiness. It was all I could do to keep from grabbing the station attendant by the shoulders and shaking her into sense, screaming, "None of it's CONSISTENT! Don't you understand?! Somebody DO SOMETHING!!"

No other explanation: I was becoming Winterized.

And if that wasn't enough, there was the

Himillsy Effect. Once home, I was decorating Easter eggs at the kitchen table on Saturday night when the H.E. prompted me to strive for a little more than the usual geometric patterns. Needing a reference, I got out the illustrated children's Bible from my room and opened it to the Gospels—Matthew. Perfect. I started with the narrow, dismissive eyes . . .

"What's that you're making, hon?" Mom was in the dining room, putting the finishing touches on our centerpiece for tomorrow's dinner: Fourteen yellow marshmallow chickens with jelly-bean eyes arranged in a Busby Berkeley formation around a ceramic rabbit-shaped vase the size of a small beatific child clutching a basket, wearing a blue buttonless blazer and sprouting five purple lilies and two palm fronds from last Sunday out of its head. All on a stage of shredded pink and seafoam green plastic grass dotted with more jelly beans and foil-wrapped chocolate eggs and chickies.

"An egg." Next I did his small, pinched mouth. Hah!—try *that* with a Q-tip and Paas vegetable dye No. 6, Michelangelo!

"I *know*. What's on it?" She was making the chickies spell out "HE IS RISEN."

"Pontius Pilate."

"Oh." She wasn't really listening. Till I knocked over the bullet-shaped bottle of red dye, inflicting a blooming wound on the table-cloth.

"GodDAMN it! Son of a bloody, Goddamned BITC—" Whoops. Forgot where I was for a sec. Uh oh.

She gasped. A mask of mortification covered her face, as she watched her only son sentence himself to yet another week, at least, in Purgatory.

"This . . . pilot . . . ," she started, her relentless sense of holiday cheer overcoming her horror of blasphemy and steering things back to the realm of the festive, ". . . is he in the air force? Why put him on an egg?"

A good question.

And I knew the answer.

. . .

Not long after returning to campus and the home stretch of the semester, I was between classes on a crisp Tuesday afternoon when I happened upon the most extraordinary thing, about twenty yards away across the mall. A boy and a girl (both maybe a few years older than me) were sitting on a bench, books at their side, having a casual conversation. Then the boy leaned to kiss her and she obliged, her hand to his face. I didn't recognize them at first because they were two people who I could tell, even from where I was standing, enjoyed each other's company.

But no mistake: it was Garnett and Himillsy.

Unnoticed, I stood gaping. Stumped. It seemed so . . . wrong. Ever since the Christmas party I'd been adding to their Hepburn-Tracy scenario in my head, except for H&G there would *never* be a third reel when they throw down their weapons, kiss, and stroll off arm in arm as the credits roll. She rarely even mentioned him when we were together. So which was the real her—G's or mine? Both? Neither?

Then I realized there was no *mine*. And knowing there wouldn't be, I went on to class.

Later that week, while rummaging through Thenson's desk drawer in desperate search of his emergency roll of Necco wafers, I came across some paperwork he'd filled out—an application to room next fall with Pompy Sugarland, a double-chinned boy from down the hall who picked his nose whenever he thought no one was looking. I should have felt betrayed, but I didn't. The things about Thenson I so initially admired—his aimlessness, his cavalier attitude about any coherent goal—were now reborn as my nemeses. He still had no idea what he wanted to do, and couldn't have cared less.

And now, thanks to Winter, I *did* . . .

• • •

... which leads us to the third formal Graphic Design critique. Our problem combined conceptual theory and practical application. "Design a poster," Winter ordered, "that gets me to either *start* doing something, or *stop* doing something."

• • •

BASIC INTERLUDE (III)

What you have to be careful to remember about Big and Small, two extremely powerful and dangerous tools, is that they can extend to infinity in either direction. If you think too hard about this, you'll go mad; though that particular problem hasn't yet seemed to afflict anyone here. Maybe you could surprise me and show up on Thursday in an incurable delirium wearing a canvas jacket with very, very long sleeves.

Consider: Big can always be bigger and Small smaller, and when in doubt they ought to be. The atom is the Universe and vice versa. And they're both identical.

Everything in between is what should concern you.

Take it, as with all things, on a case-by-case basis, and use caution. If, for example, you're promoting a local farmer with a sign and you want a tomato to look just huge, you could blow it up until the entire thing fills the picture plain and all you see is red. That would be OK, except now it probably no longer reads as a tomato. So you tilt up, and show . . . the stem, now the relative size of a houseplant. And you keep the type small. Wow. Now him *I want to go to.*

Conversely, TWA comes a-knocking, and wants a poster boasting of their powers. Why not use a shot of a lone bird—a midflight speck in a vast, sheltering sky. Have the type trailing after it, and, when I zoom in to read . . . oh . . . it's not a bird at all. A plane.

It's . . .

THE THIRD CRITIQUE.

Art 127 (Introduction to Graphic Design),
Winter Sorbeck, instr.

For which we are to design a poster, so that upon see-
ing it, the viewer will feel strangely compelled either
to start an action or cease one.

Mike went first this time. Maybe he thought it would give him an advantage, or at least a license for ceremony: he gingerly untied and parted the covers of his faux-leather portfolio case, easing out a good-sized sheet of poster board; then slowly peeled back the layer of protecting vellum. Crenck tacked his piece to the wall with an air of solemn purpose, and stood back to make sure it was straight, to admire its soaring slogan,

KEEP
AMERICA
BEAUTIFUL!

Again, like his "hot" project, the craftsmanship was excellent. With a sign painter's prefab precision, he'd produced a rolling countryside complete with barn, silo, and tractor, all polished and rounded, but with just a hint of expression from the artist's hand—sort of in the manner of Grant Wood's ex-assistant after a few scotches. The type spanned the heavens: three lines on a tilted arc—in an electric orange which hit the azure sky and vibrated almost audibly.

As did Winter. "And how are we supposed to do that, exactly?" Some sort of terrible crime had been committed here. I was baffled.

"Do what?" Mike, all innocent.

Sorbeck struggled to control himself. Jeez—what was the big deal? Was he looking at the same poster I was?

"Keep. America. Beautiful. What does that even *mean*?"

"I, it, means . . . you know . . ." Mike sounded and looked like a balloon with the air escaping.

Winter waved his hand at the work. "Does it mean canvassing the countryside with sentimental claptrap?"

Crenck, poor wretch, groped for an adequate reply. "No, I don't think—"

"Haven't we had enough of this sort of thing, Bestine?" Winter looked around the room, went over to Margaret, and picked up a textbook from the stack next to her. "May I?"

She nodded emphatically.

It was called *Titans of Industry*—one of those massive Social Studies epics that makes you just want to seize it and run for the nearest bonfire. He flipped through, found what he wanted, and ripped it out. Then he grabbed Margaret's glue pot, slathered one side of the paper, walked up to the poster, and slapped it over the meticulously rendered landscape, leaving the slogan untouched.

"Okay, everybody," he said, "It's not the right size, I know. Use your imagination."

Now the words wafted over a full-page black-and-white photo of the industrial center of Pittsburgh. Four smoke stacks—steel monolith cylinders belching soot—rose out of a sea of smog, like gun barrels from a capsized destroyer.

This changed the effect of the message completely, turning it over on itself and forging an altogether new meaning. Amazing.

"That's," squeaked Margaret, aghast, "that's horrible. How could you do that?"

"Do what?" Winter looked actor-hurt. "Build the smelting plant? Pigtails, that's America . . ."

She was obviously skeptical, appalled. "No . . ."

Sorbeck scowled, and became a snowball at the top of a mountain. He launched himself off the peak and rolled towards her, saying, ". . . and so is slavery." Gathering size, mass . . . "And lynch mobs. And the H-bomb." Growing, gaining speed . . . "And witch hunts. And murdering every Indian who gets in the way so we can build another Levittown." Obliterating everything in his path, till—*ka-blam!* "Is that *BEAUTIFUL* enough for YOU?"

"W-well, I think," Margaret managed, shaking, putting her bravest face on it, "that the poster, the way it was, before . . ."

"Yes, honey?"

". . . was good."

Winter narrowed his eyes.

"Yesss . . ." he said, in a low rumble. He walked towards her ". . . it *was*. That's the problem." I wouldn't have thought it possible, but he seemed to get even larger as he spoke. "All the other things, that I just mentioned—they used to be *good* too. Hell, a lot of people think they still are. Am I supposed to *like* that?"

No doubt—she was fatally sorry she'd spoken up. Sorry that God had ever put a tongue in her mouth.

"Pigtails, if Bestine really wants to keep America beautiful, he might consider honestly showing us what will happen if we don't, instead of trying to prove what a great illustrator he thinks he is."

Mike shrank in mortification, beyond human speech. He just sort of gurgled and tried to cease to exist.

Winter: "Kiddies, Graphic Design, if you wield it effectively, is Power. Power to transmit ideas that change everything. Power that can destroy an entire race or save a nation from despair. In this century, Germany chose to do the former with the swastika, and America opted for the latter with Mickey Mouse and Superman." He hesitated, alarmed at his own observation. "Jesus, that's worthy of a good afternoon's dissertation in itself."

Was that next?

"But do you know what's best about America?" He wasn't asking *us*. "Jackie Robinson. Frank Lloyd Wright. Billie Holiday. Albert Einstein. Cole Porter. In other words: A shine. A misogynist fop. A strung-out jigaboo. A displaced kike. A flaming *flit*. And who the hell CARES, because they're all so goddamn GREAT. They do what they do, and they're the BEST, and that's all that matters. *That's* what's *best* about America—'good' is never good enough, no matter *WHO* you are." He stopped to breathe, and leaned in to level his face against Margaret's.

"Now, Pigtails, I want you to repeat after me."

Margaret, terrified: "Y-yes?"

"Good."

"G-good."

"Is."

"I-is."

"Dead."

"D-d—"

"SAY IT!"

"Dead." She started to sob.

"Now, all together, Sunshine."

She couldn't.

He waited. "*Say* it, Pigtails."

She did what she could to pull herself together, slowly got her things in order, and walked out.

So much for Pigtails.

Winter went up to his chair in the front of the room, lit his pipe, and sat down. He was as rattled, actually, as she was.

"This class is not a pretty picture postcard . . ." He put his Zippo in his shirt pocket. ". . . it's an urgent telegram." We started to breathe again—he'd come back down to human size. Conversational. "Telegrams, by the way, if you've never seen one, are visually quite intriguing, because the static, sober typography and lack of punctuation can never accurately reflect the usually frantic and disquieting nature of the content." He took a puff. "But I digress. Bestine, you are dismissed." Mike shook himself to action, took down his poster, and sat.

Winter: "Next. D Squared."

David David went to the front. He pulled a sta-

plegun out of his army-issue kit bag, and with
nary a flinch riveted his poster to the cinder
blocks with four rifle-shot blasts, one in each corner. Two sets of words and two pictures had been
placed on the board, alternated and stacked. All
of the typography was assembled from letters cut
out of screaming tabloid headlines. The first
phrase was:

WHEN YOU
ENJOY

followed by the front of a box of raspberry Jell-
O, pasted onto the surface. Then below that,

YOU
ENJOY

accompanied by an eight-by-ten glossy color
photo of a close-up of a cow's foot, caked with
filth.

He stared at all of us with impassive distaste.

After an airless minute, Winter said, "Okay, D
Squared, I think I got it. I'll let you explain."

David David closed his eyes for a moment,
readied himself, and delivered, in not even a
monotone—a dial tone:

"Any and all gelatin products manufactured
in North America and Western Europe consist

entirely of the dismembered hooves of cows, horses, pigs, and goats, which are boiled until the blood and the dirt and the hair and the shit are washed away and the resulting sebaceous mass can be left to dry and be ground into dust and put into boxes covered with laughing people and drawings of fruit and pretty colors, for our idle pleasure. Jell-O. JuJubees. Smuckers. Gum drops. Dong Dongs: They are all the feet of the Quadruped Oppressed, trampling our hot, wet, jelly tongues, while we laugh and sing and dance . . ."

Note to self: Cut this guy a *wide* berth.

". . . as the animals, legless and screaming—"

"Alright, ALRIGHT," Winter yelled. "Point *taken*."

A girl in the back raised her hand. "Wait a minute! Is that really TRUE?" DD turned to her.

"Do you realize that your left leg contains enough tallow to produce at least four boxes of Nabisco Chew-eez Lemon Squares? And your breasts—"

"CORK IT!" shouted Winter, silencing the room. "Let's try to address the poster itself. Any comments?"

I put my arm up, disregarding my own safety. "I think it's a strong idea. But the presentation makes it a little . . . unclear."

"Thank you, Happy. Yes. While D-Squared's

information, I assume, is of impeccable accuracy, without his inimitable vocal presentation, it remains an enigma. This is not, if one were controlling the funds of some sort of Board in the Effort of Shielding the Hooved, as one would have wished. What he's done though, which is indeed graphically in the realm of the interesting, lies in his keenly selected substitution of images for words. Had he literally said, 'If you eat Jell-O, you eat a shit-smeared pig's foot,' it wouldn't have the same effect."

Hims spoke up. "So what's the best solution?"

Winter thought a moment. "Probably, I'm afraid, a television commercial. He requires the benefits of sound and movement, which unfortunately the limits of two-dimensional Graphic Design do not afford. It also wouldn't hurt to have someone who doesn't seem to be demanding a ransom handle the typography. D-Squared, you may step down, free to resume your contragelatinous crusade; and you, Girleen, while we're at it, may come forward."

Himillsy made her way up, lugging something heavy covered with a plastic tarp. She unwrapped and pulled out a piece of crumpled sheet metal about two-and-a-half feet wide and three feet tall. It was all she could do to hoist it onto the chalk ledge and let it land against the wall with a clang. It read,:

NO PARKING
7 AM - 5 PM
MON THRU FRI
VIOLATORS
WILL BE TOWED
AT OWNER'S
EXPENSE

There were two nasty gashes in it—one at the top and one at the bottom—both centered. She seemed pleased.

Winter did not. "Darlin', Christ on a bicycle! You were supposed to design it your*self!*"

Himillsy, suddenly furious, at the top of her lungs: "I *altered* it! It *used* to be on a pole! I made it my *own!*"

"Girleen," Sorbeck was rubbing his eyes, at wit's end, "when are you going to decide to do some *work?*"

"I'm sorry?" Hims practically threw thunderbolts. "When was the last time *you* climbed onto the roof of your car in wedgies, with nothing but a Phillips screwdriver and a ball-peen hammer, to rip a five-pound sheet of tin from the base of a streetlight at four o'clock in the morning?" She was breathless. "*Without* getting arrested? If that's not work, Mr. Chips, then enlighten me, forsooth, what is?"

"Thinking up your own idea, girlygirl. Not the township's."

"What about *Duchamp*?"

"What about him?"

"Well, he said a piss pot was Art, and Shazzam! it was Art. I say, Shazzam! This sign is Graphic Design!"

"And it is! Kazowie! The Traffic Department's!"

This was going nowhere. I felt like ringing a bell and sending them both back to their corners.

I raised my hand again. "Er, excuse me, but isn't at least the basic concept true to the assignment? I mean, except it sort of does both—it makes you do something by not doing it."

"Nice try, Hap." Winter snapped, "She's got *you* on a short leash, doesn't she?"

Now wait a minute.

"Alright, enough of this. Girleen, go back to the Armory Show." He motioned for her to sit. "One more. Maybelleen?"

Hims flounced back to her seat, fuming.

Maybelle walked to the front of the room as if the floor might give way any second and send her plummeting to the basement.

Up went her poster. She'd had it printed by a local carnival show-print letter press shop. Big black wood-type letters were set against a rainbow split font background that was yellow at the top and faded to orange, red, purple, and finally blue, at the bottom.

It said:

WHATEVER
YOU DO,
DON'T
THINK OF
ELEPHANTS!

Oh, no.

"It's something my grandfather used to say," she offered, meekly. "It always made me . . . think of . . ." she trailed off and looked to her feet. I thought she might launch into some idiotic story rife with needless detail about Grandpa Lee and his short but triumphant years with Ringling Bros., but she wisely clammed up. Maybe she was starting to learn something.

Winter squinted and went up to the poster. He lowered his head and shook it slightly. Then he lifted his left leg up to his chest and brought his foot down with a thud onto the desk in front of Maybelle. She jumped. He slowly untied his shoe, removed it, and took off his sock. He did the same with his right foot. Weird.

We all held our breath. Frankly, I wasn't in the mood to hear Winter chew Maybelle out again— it was a little too much like watching someone smack a puppy that just didn't know when to stop barking. Really: wasn't Mike and Margaret's blood enough for one crit?

Mabes, who in this room was never far from tears anyway, started to tremble and . . .

"Here," he put his socks into her hands, "these are for you." He forced her fingers into fists, made her claim them. "Darlin', do you know why?" She brought herself to look at him, and made ready for the next scathing tirade.

"Because those pachyderms . . ." he said, softly, with reverence, ". . . that you let loose in my head," he became so sweet, so beautiful, "just knocked 'em *right* off."

And she fell into him, and she cried.

Her shock: realizing she had never, ever in her life, lost herself to tears because she was *happy*. It really was possible to cry because she had done something right. Because she didn't screw it all up. It was all, in her own words from last semester, so new. "God, it will never happen again," she must have thought as she drained her ducts into Winter's argyles.

Oh, what I wouldn't have done to be crying into those socks.

Anyway, he gently propped Maybelle's quivering form against the wall, ripped off her poster, and went to the window. Energized, he threw it open and barked at some hapless passerby, "Hey!"

We heard a muffled "What?"—an older man's voice. Winter thrust the poster out into space.

"Look at this!"

A beat, then Sorbeck asked, "So? What does it make you think of?"

"Uh, elephants?"

"RIGHT! Hah! Go AWAY!"

He pulled it back in and faced us. Intoxicated.

"You SEE? POWER!"

He reflexively beat his fist against the window, cracking the pane. He did it again. We heard a shower of glass hit the pavement.

"Do you SEE?"

• • •

Thank you, God: I wasn't called on to show mine. Winter would have used it for toilet paper, and rightly so. I won't even go into what it was. I destroyed it as soon as I got out of the room.

• • •

"What a load of crap. You'd think we were taking Drama. Like, like rehearsing act *three* of some bozo Arthur Miller play—one that waves the flag it's pissing on." Hims was on the boil like I'd never seen, as we walked at a good clip down the mall after class, on the way to town.

I gently antagonized her. "You're just sore because he handed you your head." And made Maybelle Queen for a Day—who could have seen *that* coming?

"Horse hockey! I think he actually *buys* that genius schmenius line." I watched the dusk fall on her face. "He can go pound sand! How often has history heard that story? It's a *joke*. Graphic Design is going to save the goddamn world just as soon as Christianity, penicillin, and democracy do. Superman saved the US of A? Gee, that'll be news to my Uncle Osborne. He was at D day." She was really hitting stride, all the rejoinders she either didn't think of in class—or didn't quite have the nerve to voice—pouring out of her. God, I loved it. A good Himillsy rant was like a Callas aria without the restraint. "Lady Day got a free ride cause she's a *canary*? I guess that's why Carnegie Hall just *welcomed* her with *open* goddamn doors! Jesus Jehosephat! Sawbuck wants to trade one Levittown for another—of his own liking. He trots out the pantheon of disenfranchised genius so he can add his own goddam name to the list—the next two-bit wizard from the sticks. It's just another cliché about America, and maybe it's the worst one of all, because people like him—in *Power*, still believe in it." She caught her breath. "Besides—Joe Louis is cuter, and knows how to kiss."

"You sucked *face* with Joe Louis?"

"Don't change the subject."

"Sorry. So . . . you *liked* Mike's poster, then."

We stopped. Main Street buzzed behind her like gnats around a licorice whip as she grimaced, weary of my idiocy. Of everybody's.

"Christ, of *course* not."

· · ·

My Black Thursday, that day of days, started innocently enough. Eggs Benedict at the dining hall. A-minus on a Geo Sci quiz. Booster burger at the Caf with Thenson for lunch.

Then, that afternoon, in the middle of GD, when we were going over the history and use of Futura and bracing ourselves for the fourth critique assignment, I attempted to enjoy a stick of gum.

Mistake of the century.

The irony in this, and what followed, is: I *hate* gum. If David David thought mere last names turned us all into cows, he had nothing on gum. Anyway, Maybelle had offered me a piece and I thought it would be impolite not to accept. As I began to pop it into my mouth, Winter stopped in midsentence.

"Happy, what are you doing?"

Shit. "H-having a piece of gum." This *was* supposed to be College after all, were we not finally free to—

"Really. What brand?"

Didn't even remember. I smoothed out the wrapper. "Um, Wrigley's Doublemint."

"You were going to throw the wrapper away, weren't you?"

Oh no. Out for blood. Why? "Not. Necessarily."

"Then why did you crumple it up?"

Shitshitshit. Hot. Pulse gaining. "Because I—"

"DON'T bother, Happy." All eyes were on me, the new sacrifice. Winter sharpened his knives. "I guess you just don't think it's beautiful enough for your refined *taste*."

"I hadn't even thought—"

"No, you hadn't. Take a look at it."

The familiar green background, the black double arrow, the simple red sans-serif type, the laurel crown of mint leaves. I guess it *was* kind of beautiful. I'd just never thought to regard it. And why should I have to? Why was I being singled out?

"Happy, who designed it?"

"I . . . don't know."

"Hey kiddies!" Winter was asea in his own squall, taking us all along for the ride and making me walk the plank. "There's something Happy doesn't know! Aren't we *excited*?"

What, in God's own hell, brought this on?

"Well, Happy, your mission, if you ever want to set foot in this room again, is to find out, and report from the field. You see fit to chew the gum, but couldn't give a tinker's damn about the poor son of a bitch who has to figure out what it looks like, only so you can cast his efforts onto the trash heap."

"I don't even chew—"

x

"IF I WANT YOUR OPINION, I'LL BEAT IT OUT OF YOU!"

Horror, in my heart. I won't cry. I will. Not. Cry.

He stomped over to Mike, picked up the small paper bag on the desk in front of him. He dumped the pencils in it onto the table and threw the bag, empty, at me.

"Here! Design your way out of THAT!"

Didn't cry. Honest.

Until I picked up the bag.

• • •

When the air cleared, we got the assignment for the fourth crit—the weirdest yet. He was careful not to look at me as he issued our orders, an un-gesture that hurt more than a piercing stare ever would. We had to show Winter "something that I've never seen before and will never be able to forget. Because that should always be your goal. If you can do that, you can do anything—never attempt anything less."

• • •

Maybelle, who felt responsible for my plight (because she *was*, thanks) insisted on tagging along with us to the Diner. Hims let her, for my sake—a giant sacrifice, I knew—and they both, in their own way, tried to console me. Kind of sweet, actually, though it only brought the threat of more tears.

"I am so, so sorry. I'll never chew it again," Mabes cooed. "He doesn't mean it. He's just upset. Of course you can come to the next class." As if it were up to her. Ridiculous.

"Not without finding out who designed the bloody Doublemint wrapper," I moped.

"Can you?"

"I'll *try*. Jesus, whoever it was is probably dead and gone. Who'll even know? Why is he doing this to me?"

Hims chimed in. "Wrong place, wrong time. It's his whole unsung invisible architects of the modern world routine, it's not *you*." She opened the door to the Diner. "And what are you so worked up about? God, you're free! I'd *pay* for my walking papers from that zipperhead."

Once we were in a booth, Mills continued to try and cheer me up, using Maybelle as bait.

"So dear," she asked her, "what do you have in mind for the next crit? Sounds like a hard one."

"Goodness," Mabes responded, "haven't even thought about it, what with all the upset."

"Well, this idea is free: you should do what I was going to do. I was going to stand on the table, lift up my dress, and release a flock of rose-colored doves from my vagina. They'd circle, form the words 'GO STATE!' in midair, and fly back in. But Erbie's just didn't stock enough pink dye. Maybe you could pull some strings I couldn't. Or use blue—they had plenty. Goes with your coloring. S'cuse." And she was off to the ladies'.

"Everything she says," Maybelle's eyes went into her coffee, another trust broken, "has a pin in it. Even the nice things." Then she looked at me. "She *was* trying to be nice, wasn't she?"

When Mills came back to the booth, we'd changed the subject to Mike, who, I'd be the first to admit, had troubles in GD that I'd not ever had to face.

"Thick as a brick, sorry," said Hims. "That boy is the distance between two points."

Maybelle took up his cause. "Well, I admire him. We talked some, that day on the bus. He's from Boalsburgh. Used to be a commercial sign painter, and decided he wanted more out of life. Scrimped and saved for years to come here. He's thirty-one, can you imagine? And Winter treats him so *shabbily* . . ."

"Darling, here's one thing I've heard, and I believe it: After age twenty-five, you're not a victim anymore—you're a volunteer."

"I still think it's inspiring. And why not? Look

at Grandma Moses—she was well into her sixties before *she* started painting."

Himillsy was practically rutzing. "Sorry, dear, but I've seen the work. She never started *painting*."

. . .

After an hour's wait in line, my call from the dorm's hall pay phone to the Wrigley office, in Chicago, was yielding the foreseen dead results. I tried to ignore the hot stares of the guys behind me as I got handed on the other line from department to department, and finally reached someone in Package Production.

"Yes? What can I do for you?"

"I need to find out who originally designed the label for Doublemint gum. I need a name."

"Wow. Now *there's* a question. Hold please?"

"Sure."

Five minutes passed like kidney stones. I read up for my Geo Sci final. Fed fifty cents to the machine.

"Hi. Sorry."

" 'S okay."

"It was handled by a firm outside the company. A good twenty-plus years ago it seems, sorry to say."

"And, the name of the company?"

"Gee. Got me there. Hold again?"

"Yep."

Six minutes this time, onto Ab Psych, more nickels, more hostility.

"Hi. You there?"

"I am."

"Just wanted to get everything straight before I got back on."

"Thanks."

"It seems it was an agency in Connecticut. New Haven. Outfit name of Spear, Rakoff, and Ware. They're still around. Here's the number—"

At least it was something. "Just one more call . . . " I said meekly, and it was ringing.

"Dear, slack off your cares."

"Excuse me?" Was I hearing things? A muffled guffaw in the background? Then, seriously,

"Spear, Rakoff, and Ware. How may I deflect your call?"

Deflect ? "Um, can I have, what—the Design Department?"

"God, you certainly *can*. Hold." Wiseguy receptionist. Probably blotto.

"Art Department."

"Hi. Please . . . please don't hang up. I'm a design student at State U? I need to find out who designed the Doublemint gum package. For a school project."

"Ah," a blurry exchange in the background, then, "We did?"

"Well, yes. But who specifically? I need a name, for a paper I'm writing."

"That was what—" He checked. "Twentysome years ago? I just started last June. Sketchy Spear'd know. Been here forever."

"Can I speak with him?"

"At lunch. Peppe's. God knows when we'll see 'im."

"When's a good time to call back?"

"He's here late."

"How late?"

• • •

At eight-thirty, I went to the pay phone in the Baxter building, outside of 207 (kick me: should have done gone there in the first place) with two rolls of nickels. Pulled up a chair. Tried again, and while I waited for someone to pick up, I stared at the door to the classroom, vowing to walk through it again as soon as—

"Art Department." Grandpa Kettle voice.

"Can I have Mr. Spear, please?"

"Speakin'."

Capital. I tried to stay calm. "Er, you don't know me, but I'm a design student. I need your help."

"Heh. All ears."

"Great. My professor at State U gave me an assignment for a project at school . . . I need to find out who made the original label for Wrigley's Doublemint gum. Who designed it."

"Jeez, that's a while back."

"I know, I'm sorry. I was told you're the only one could help me."

"Heh, well. See, Lars Rakoff, he's dead now. But he was the big cheese at the time. He did it."

I didn't believe him. "You sound—doubtful."

"Heh, no."

I figured it out.

"It was you, wasn't it?"

"What's this for? You with the papers?"

"No, just a student. I think graphic designers just don't get enough credit, and I want to set the record straight."

"Heh." A moment. "I did the green for the background, not exactly a leap. Then I tried—two mint leaves. Didn't fly. But the double arrow, and the type, came from this kid we had here. Not even a year. He really snapped the crackers. Uh, big guy. Football, maybe. Ladies' man, heh. Smart as a whip, lotsa ideas, I remember. Wasn't gonna last *long*. Jeezus Pete, his name was . . . what? Serbock? Winston? . . .

" . . . Hello?"

I caught my breath. "Winter. Sorbeck."

"That's him! Say, you know'im? Hadn't thoughta those days in *years*. Just a kid myself. That whole Doublemint business, we had no *idea . . .*"

"You've been, so. So helpful. Can't thank you enough, really. Could you . . . possibly send me your business card? First-class postage? I'll pay."

"Heh. Pleasure . . ."

I gave him the address.

Supposed to meet Hims at the Skeller, nine sharp. Boy, did I need that beer.

• • •

"Son. Of. A. Bitch." She was very, very impressed. Waving her cig like a magic wand, left and right, over my head, christening me. "Sherlock, Sunuvabitch, Holmes."

"I'm lucky, is what. Can you imagine the odds? The guy still alive, still working there, answering the phone? Remembering?"

"Outrageous. We should have guessed. Explains everything—no wonder that psycho went bananas. Get him on the *couch*, ASAP."

"I'm just relieved. Seemed like such a personal attack. Couldn't understand it." I brought up the coming crit, putting myself back in the race. Felt *great.* "Old guy's sending me his business card—it'll be my piece for the crit. It's had to have changed, at least a little, since Sorbeck was there, so technically he's never seen it before. Ought to shake him up, right?"

"Brill. Really."

"Think? How about you, sans the flock?"

"Couple ideas. Nothing vocable."

"It'll come."

"Always does."

We ordered another round.

And another.

Then, the unthinkable.

"HapEEE! And GirLEEEEN! My Ideeeeeals!!"

No, not here. This was our Batcave. The Joker *never* gets into the Batcave.

He lumbered towards us, a large shape emerging, out of the Skeller murk.

Roaring. Breath combustible. Levi's, a kelly green Lacoste and a khaki windbreaker. Planted himself across from me and next to Mills, who was dying.

She croaked, "As a matter of fact, we were *just* leaving—"

"Kiddies! What'll ya have! Round's on me." Winter seemed so happy to see us, I couldn't even talk.

Hims: "Jar. Of Rolling Rock."

"Two."

He sprang up to get them.

She glared. "Beyond the bleeding pale. A coupla Jacks and he's Santa Claus? We shoulda poured it in his pipe before crit. Where's the *zipperhead* who ate and shat you out this afternoon in a single gulp?" She didn't wait for an answer. "*Shit.* I'm gone."

"Wait! Stay! When'll we get this chance again?"

"Never, please."

"*Stay.* For the Wrigley evening *news.*"

A breath. "You're not going to save it for crit?"

"This is too good to pass up. Besides, he'll never remember it anyway."

She seemed . . . strange–frightened? No, never. "Okay. Ten minutes. That's it."

He came back with the beers and another Jack D– neat, in a beaker.

Hims went into Nanette Fabray mode. "So, where's Mrs. Sorbeck tonight? Sewing circle?"

A dark chortle. "Darlin', wish I knew. She made me her *was*band a long time ago. After giving me many a wood shampoo."

"Sorry to hear it."

I changed the subject, lickety-split, feeling like Edward R. Murrow interviewing the first Martian in captivity. "Uh, where did you teach before here?"

"Heh. Everywhere. Yale first, and the longest. Helped start the program. With Albers."

Whoever that was. "Really. Why'd you leave?"

"Hurmm. Complicated. Him, mostly. You know all those squares he does?"

Hadn't a clue. "Yeah?"

"Those are side views of his head."

"I see."

Himillsy moved the conversation to art theory. "Speaking of which, I have a new, definitive axiom, about sculpture," she announced. We were all ears. "If you can set a drink on it, it's good. If you can set two drinks on it, it's better."

Winter snickered. "So, Joseph Cornell . . . ?"

"God's *own*."

"And Brancusi . . ."

"Worthless!"

"Waitaminute!" I protested. "What about Rodin?"

She didn't miss a beat. "They all have *bases*, don't they?"

"Girly, think ya *got* somethin' there."

I felt emboldened by drink. "Uh, Winter?"

"Shoot." He took a pull on the mash.

"I, just wanted to tell you."

He swallowed . . .

"Sketchy Spear says hi."

. . . and choked. "Huk!" He wiped his mouth. "Well, I'll be god*damned*."

Those eyes, back on me, where they belonged. Unbearable, diamond-blue drills.

"You *are* a magician, Hap! My ideal!"

Could have stared at them till I was Swiss cheese . . .

• • •

Two hours and three rounds later, we were somehow onto Matisse. I didn't have much to offer, except a snippet I'd read in *Life* magazine: "He wasn't much on discourse. Once said, 'Painters must begin by cutting out their tongues.'"

"Sheesh—why stop *there*?" Winter slurred, "If he would've done his hands next, all those innocent little pieces of paper could've been *spared*."

Hims was hooting. "Ha! It's so, so *true*! You sound like Clement Greenberg!"

"CLEMENT GREENBERG?! I HATE Clement Greenberg!"

"What's wrong with him?" she dared.

"The problem with Clement Greenberg," he was fading fast, "is that when God put teeth in his mouth, he ruined a perfectly good ASSHOLE."

And he was out, head on chest. Check please.

"Charming," Hims hissed.

"Last call." Greck made the rounds.

"Well, we're off." She shouldered her bag.

"We can't just leave him here," I pleaded.

"Oh, I think he sort of goes with the decor."

"Hims, I'm serious."

She swiveled. "After what he did to you, this afternoon? To *me*? I wouldn't piss down his throat if his heart was on *fire*." She motioned for me to hightail it. I was crestfallen—we were having such a good time.

Mills was baffled with me, disgusted. "The grade can't mean *that* much."

"It's not the *grade*. Jesus."

She went for the stairs. "Right. The Dodd Express is pulling out. All aboard. Toot toot." Gone.

"Hims . . ."

Greck came up to me.

"I know where his wheels are." He nodded to Winter's broken form. "Ya want a hand?"

"Really would. Thanks." Maybe if I got him to his car, he could snap to and get home, wherever that was.

Greck lifted Winter with a *Huff!* and hauled him, amazingly, upstairs. I trailed. Mills had vamoosed.

Damn it. She really left me.

"You gonna drive?" Greck asked. He was skeptical, to say the least.

It hadn't even occurred to me. "Suppose I am."

He stuffed Sorbeck into the passenger seat and headed back down the stairs before I could thank him again. I looked at the car, not quite believing—a Jaguar two seater, almost as small as Himillsy's Corvair—talk about ten pounds of potatoes in a five-pound bag. I sat, Winter spilling over next to me, and got acclimated. Pulled the seat front. I'd driven a standard before, once—cousin Sal's Ford. How different could this be?

Greck had gotten me the keys from Winter's pocket and the address from his driver's license—west side of town, didn't know it at all. Stopped at the Shell for directions.

Finally on our way, the stratospheric absurdity sank in, with all its implications: I'm in his car, driving, by fits and starts. He's unconscious, and on this day of days, totally dependent . . . on *me*.

IF I WANT YOUR OBLIVION, I'LL DRIVE IT INTO YOU! Fate was playing pinball with me, but so what. It felt *good*—whoops! Wrong word. It felt better than that, it—

"Jew baller yet?"

Almost swerved into a ditch. "P-pardon?"

Eyes shut, not moving. But awake. "The pixie. *Jew* baller?"

Good heavens. "No."

"I did."

Somehow, I kept my eyes on the road; my hands obeyed me—despite their better judgment—and clutched the wheel instead of his throat. Jealousy hot and crippling. Jealous of whom, actually?

"Not worth it. A lunger. Screamed like a cat in a bag . . . " And he was out again. Sawing wood.

And I remembered, back at the Skeller, just now—the coda to something Himillsy said.

After what he did to you, this afternoon?
        To me?

Pig. You *pig.*

• • •

I finally found the house—only passed it three times. *Very* hard to see—a box ranch model— almost completely overtaken with ivy, no lights on. The driveway: a perilous drop, garage at the finish line. No thanks. I parked on the street in front. With an arm like a yoke over my shoulder, I barely managed to drag him to the door. The keys for the house and the car, thank God, were on the same ring. Once in, I snapped on a light.

Yowza.

After a trip down the main hallway that would have felled a boot camp marine, I got him to the bedroom and plopped him down. Then I caught my breath and went on safari. Several rooms were filled with boxes—still packed. But the living room and kitchen and den were all set up. I clicked on another lamp. Spectacular: one face of the double-height living room was covered with old game boards, none of which I recognized. I went up close to one to find the manufacturer and discovered it was . . . a painting. On wood, as were the rest.

The wall thirty feet or so across from it was a floor-to-ceiling array of glass shelves holding water pitchers, which shamed you with the realization that you never seriously considered before what water pitchers could look like, that they really could attain the grace of futurist sculpture without the pretension. He must have traversed the globe to collect them all. I gingerly took one down: a glazed Lilliputian streamlined skyscraper, handle where the extension's penthouse would be. I turned it over—just a small stamp, plain letters: WS. He had . . . cast it himself. I examined three more. All WS.

He'd made all of them. Forty, easily.

In the room's corners, Depression-era five and dime display cases held battalions of tin robots. Silent sentries in all sizes. Hundreds.

I thought: Garnett should see this. It's ordered, it's not confining, it's different. But it's *comfortable,* and minimal in its own way—it didn't seem cluttered or busy because the other two white walls, save for large black cubical leather sofas (one of which held a calico cat twice the size of Colonel Percy, asleep and purring), were virtually untouched and provided oases of blank space for the eye to rest upon. You could sit and look at it all for *hours.*

"Whoozzatt."

Oh, my Christ.

He lurched in the doorway, squinting, in the weak light. Undershirt, shorts. A magnificent shipwreck.

I said, loudly, "I-it's me. It's alright. You're home."

He blinked.

"I brought you *home*." Might as well have been speaking Esperanto. I pointed to the wall. "The game boards, you made them?"

He struggled to respond. "Grad thesis, twenties." Whether his twenties or the century's wasn't clear. He coughed miserably, disgust published all over his face, as if he couldn't bear the sight of them. "Pritt. Tee," he spat.

I looked again at the luminous wall of diagrammatic color and shape—a playland mosaic dedicated to the ultimate rainy afternoon's distraction. Each unique, but they blended into a seamless symphony of hue, type, line, system: clowns, fire trucks, monsters, playgrounds, witches, rocket ships, animals of every type—all taken apart and reconfigured, invaded by geometry and rules of abstraction. It was impossible to imagine them ever separated. Such carefree regiment, so urgent in their frivolity. So . . . whimsically diabolical. If only life could be this way—this figured out, with the goals so clear.

"They're more than that, and you know it. Or

you wouldn't have made them in the firs–" I turned back to him.

Not there. I went into the bedroom.

Collapsed. Flat on his back. Snoring.

I was about to turn the light out and go on exploring when the great graphic design gods took pity on me and tapped my shoulder.

"Idiot! Look! On the sideboard!"

A Polaroid camera . . . like Dad's. With flash, tripod, and film. Oh, I *couldn't.*

"You only live once!"

"But what if he wakes up?" I implored them, "That's it, the end! I'm through!"

"Ya takes yer chances, kid!'"

And they were gone.

I crept up to Winter's bulk. It rose and ebbed with each hoggy wheeze.

"Winter," I said, not quietly, next to his ear.

"Can you hear me?" Nothing. A final test: I *had* to.

Oh, please don't move.

I lifted up my hands and in single instant brought them together in front of his face with a sickening *smack!*

Held my breath.

Dead to the world. Wow: Jesus *was* my pal. I got onto the bed, taking the plunge–God, I hadn't even dared *dream* of this. Off with my shirt. Straddled him.

My face over his—a statue's, the marble all the more beautiful for the cracks and splits. The tiny veins mapping the perfect nose, the lightning bolt valleys radiating from each eye's outer corner. I was exploring the moon—so used to it so far away for so long and now I've landed. On the Moon God. The gravity was different here—nearly none. Our lips touched. His: warm leather.

He stopped snoring.

Holy, holy shit.

I didn't move. He didn't either, just made a small noise. Regular breathing. I told myself: If he wakes up now, he'll still be drunk. I can tell him he'd lapsed into a coma and I'm giving him mouth to mouth. Barechested.

(Cut me some slack—it was a little *tense*.) My eyes went to the bedside clock. I let a minute pass.

A minute, in this situation, is an *era*.

I decided: onward. My tongue coaxed his lips, and they parted, the curtains lifting on my command performance. The jaw, already slack from the snoring, unhinged itself and I descended. My tongue met his, slid, and came to rest.

The taste became the smell became the touch. It was all there, somewhere—sweat, age, skin, strength, whiskey, flesh, salt, hair, coffee, teeth, the sweet cream of the pipe tobacco, the earthy musk of sleep. Him. I was . . . *in* him.

He who'd christened me and so now I was: Happy, in the Forbidden Planet.

The breath from his nose whistled and whipped innocently around my ear. Delicious. I held it a beat more. God, so this is what it was like. I slowly, reluctantly withdrew. Sighed. I didn't have forever. I went and got the camera. Loaded the film. Was I really doing this?

Yes.

To the guy who designed the Wrigley's God-damn Doublemint gum wrapper. To the guy who destroyed me today. I half wondered if this was what it was like for Himillsy.

No, because *I'm* in control. This is what it was like for *him*.

Trembling fingers—wouldn't yours?—grabbed the waistband of his shorts, stretched, and pulled.

They came off almost as easily as Mr. Peppie's.

Oh, *wow* . . .

• • •

I sat in the Jag for over an hour, to nearly daybreak.

In a mist of my own delirium, still trying to believe it, trying to compose myself; waiting for it to clear.

I've done the impossible.

I've disarmed you, Winter Sorbeck. From now on, whatever you say to me, I will look at you and see it in quotation marks.

The first pair will be your lips, askew; the second, *mine.*

• • •

BASIC INTERLUDE (IV)

Left to Right, Top to Bottom, Big and Small; on a two-dimensional plane, all of these tools rely on a relative truth. Now we come to In Front Of and In Back Of, which for us are big, fat lies. Very useful though, and the first of many at your disposal.

If you want A to appear to be in front of B, you have several options. You can make A much larger than B (thank you, Big and Small). You can up the ante by throwing A out of focus. And, most important, you can have A overlap B. If you don't think all of this is extraordinary, you are banished from this room. Consider: You are seducing the enemy into accepting something that isn't real and doesn't exist. If you don't think that's a valuable skill, just ask the kind folks at the Vatican how it's working for them.

In Front Of and In Back Of bring to mind a book called Flatland, *which you will be required to read by next week. In it, Edwin A. Abbott describes a world that exists only in two dimensions (ours exists in three, in case you hadn't noticed)—length and width. Its inhabitants are geometric shapes that only see each other as lines of varied color and light—a cross-section, as it were, of their "bodies." They* assume themselves as superior to the poor wretches in Lineland, who have only a point cross-section to deal with and can never get ahead of whoever is in front of them.

So we sit here in the third dimension—Spaceland—and scoff at Flatland, pitying its immeasurably thin folk because we can see it in a way they never can. But—and this is a big BUT—doesn't that mean that someone sits in Timeland (AKA the fourth dimension) and feels the same about us? And someone sits in the fifth watching them, and so on, as they say, into infinity?

There. Wrap your mind around **that**.

THE FOURTH CRITIQUE.

Art 127 (Introduction to Graphic Design),
Winter Sorbeck, instr.

During which we shall present to the instructor an image that he has never before seen, and will never be able to forget.

There's a special feeling (I only experienced it one other time) when you're in an un-winnable war, and you're supposed to get creamed, but you just *know* you have impenetrable armor and the perfect weapon. The whole David and Goliath bit. Truman must have felt it when he dropped the A-bomb, and I was about to join him.

I should have been scared shitless by this crit, and, okay, I was, but not for the regular reasons. Mine was the fear of succeeding to a detrimental excess.

Mike went first again, eager to earn another Retarded Martyr Merit Badge.

A disaster. I'll spare you the details.

Oh all right, quick: He held up a small . . . American flag in shades of brown (?) which, he announced, was knitted by his grandmother. Probably thought this would cover the previously lauded America and grandparent angles.

Winter: "And what makes *that* so unforgettable?"

"S-she made it all out of her own hair."

At least Sorbeck didn't waste a lot of time destroying it. In fact, he said, "Dreadful. And for you, Bestine, that's a quantum leap. Congrats."

David David brought up a plastic sandwich bag. Inside was a small turdlike nugget. Had we come to this? Winter held it to the light.

"*Seen* mushrooms before, Deedee."

"Not like this one. Pop it in your mouth, lay back. We'll talk."

Suddenly, he seemed to know what Dave D was referring to, and put it carefully in his shirt pocket.

"Later. Sit."

Maybelle's turn. But she hadn't shown up today.

"And where's Maybelleen?" Winter seemed to actually miss her. "She finally decide to cut bait?

Pity. Girl was starting to show promise. Well, on to the next . . ."

My cue. I took the whistle out of my pocket. Blew.

The door flew open.

Our Mabes, arms aloft—an acid yellow showgirl, in ostrich feathers and a sequined one piece. Her voice was a needle dragged across a Puccini record at top volume.

"I had a dream! A . . . a dream about *you*, baby!"

Goodness, those *thighs*.

Winter was suitably appalled.

Truth to tell, I pulled her aside on Saturday and put her up to all of it, because I realized that Himillsy's goof the first day was legit: he *did* want theater, and the South in Maybelle had always been pure theater anyway. I swore it was her only chance.

Though maybe the eight-cylinder motorcycle *was* a bit much. I guess Erbie couldn't come through with the scooter.

"It's gonna come *true*, baby!"

She gave it the gas and started it up, just as Erb showed her. Then she revved the engine. Liking it.

"Gonna come *through*!"

No. Don't do that.

"Get off of my runway!" *BRROOOOOOM!*

Winter, at the top of his lungs: "Stop! Okay!"

"What?!" She jerked forward to hear above the engine.

The kick stand fell and she was off.

"AAAAAAAAAAAAHHHHHH!"

Not in the plan. She was never supposed to become mobile.

Luckily, she was still in neutral and going all of three miles an hour when he managed to stop her and turn off the ignition.

Maybelle was huffing and puffing, breathless.

"H-how was that?"

Sorbeck plucked one of the feathers and mopped his forehead.

"Seen worse. B plus."

"Whew!" Eyebrows arched, "Will you remember it?"

He closed his eyes against the question.

" 'Fraid so."

Me: "I think it's only fair to warn you, we should do this in private." Yeah, *again*! Ha!

"Why?"

"I really don't want to say. You'll understand when you see it."

"Nonsense. We don't have time for games."

I'd mounted the Polaroid on a piece of five-by-seven inch poster board, with a protecting flap of black construction paper. Just now I realized that it should have been plain, brown wrapping instead. Rats. I held it up.

"It's small," I said, as he approached. Dare I add it? *Oh go ahead.* "The *picture* is, anyway."

He took it, lifted the paper covering.

Bingo.

"What?!"

Power! I can do ANYTHING.

Of course, he *had* seen it before. But not from this angle, his face in the background. Not with me smiling next to it.

He looked at the photo just long enough to accept it wasn't bogus and jammed it into his pocket, before anyone else, Lord forbid, could see.

"We'll discuss this later, Hap." Clipped. Face liver red. Wouldn't look at me. "Five o'clock. My office. Be seated."

It's a date. Aces—I was really on top.

Himillsy's turn next. The hell with *her.* She was still in my bow-wow house.

Don't Even Bother, Miss Molecule.

Okay, she looked *great*: in a size zero custard summer wool suit with black trim that Coco Chanel would have *killed* her to get the pattern for; the matching hip-level leather accessory bag with linguine shoulder strap, the simple but stellar chrome earings, the ebony kid gloves that accented her hair and with it formed a triad of deathless perfection. Hims had made all of it. Christ, why didn't she major in *fashion*?

"Ready?" She handed him a strip of five and dime photobooth pictures of herself, holding white horizontal cards. Small.

He squinted at it. "You're yanking my chain, Girly."

"Then you're not *getting* it," she said. "Look closer."

He put on his reading glasses. Each card had a word. Four panels total.

As he strained to make sense of it, she brought something metal out of the bag, gleaming chrome (it matched her *earrings*!!), and leveled it at his chest. Silence seized everyone.

The cards: 1. Don't 2. Look 3. Now 4. !!!

When I realized what she intended, you'd assume that my first thought would have been Jesus! or Yikes! or Duck!, but it wasn't. It was Wow, where'd she get one so *beautiful*? My second thought (okay, first and a half) was Jesus!

Winter, oblivious, gave in.

"Sorry, darlin'. Time's up." he said, and let the picture fall. Then he saw it. She smirked and nodded, as if to say, "Yup!"

And fired.

Deafening. Put the motorcycle to shame. I'd never heard a gun go off before, except in the movies. This was much, much different—there's just no way they can duplicate that in a theater. Remember, Chez 207 was made of concrete and had no rugs or curtains. My eyes watered from the shock, and I was deaf for the next five seconds. I just watched Winter land against the wall, which, though soundless, registered with an impact that knocked my pencils to the floor and left my teeth rattling. He slid down, in disbelief, his hands tight to his chest. He was breathing like a freight train approaching a stop. Eyes pinched.

I admit, I was looking for blood. Couldn't see any. People started to stir, startled. Confusion and smoke, as Himillsy stood firm and returned the revolver to her bag. She didn't even bother to blow on the barrel—too cliché. My ears were opening up.

Then Winter, like Lazarus, rose. Untouched. Dazed and gasping, but fine. Himillsy was saying something to him. I shook my head to get it.

". . . careful what you ask for." Smoothing her hair, which didn't need it. "Now, as soon as you forget *that*," she went to her seat, "you just let me know."

• • •

"Oh, don't make such a big *deal* out of it." Hims plunged into her burger—victory dinner at the Diner. Despite her protests, I detected a sense of relish other than the one in her mouth.

"Really, where did you *get* it?"

"Drama Department, natch." She swallowed. "I just went and filled out a green rec and submitted it to Props. Said I was doing my own production of *Death of a Salesman*. At least I didn't lie."

"There's no gun in *Death of a Salesman*."

"I know. Good thing Susie Sign-Out missed opening night."

"Amazing. I'll never forget the look on his face."

"Me too. Especially when Maybelleen became a Ziegfeld Zombie and *you* showed him whatever it was. Spill."

I didn't like scolding her, really, but I let her have it. "I wouldn't have to if I wasn't abandoned at the Skeller. You could have been in on it. Thanks a *lot*." Of course my complaints were all for show—thank *God* she went AWOL.

"Oh, soak your *head*." A lopsided smile.

And I was grinning too. Sheesh—how did she *do* that to me?

I told her all about the house, wondering how much of it was old news to her.

Left out the "conversation" in Winter's car.

And the photo session. Said I'd swiped the pic off his bedroom desk—a photo of one of his cats.

Might have been too, if I'd thought to include them.

She was disappointed. "I would have taken a whiz on his toothbrush." Which meant she probably had. "Well," she sighed, "at least the class is finally starting to get *interesting*. Soreback'll think twice about giving that one again. We were the only three that aced it."

"And David David."

"Maybe. Mr. *Mirth*." She allowed him, for a moment, into her thoughts. "I hear he used to have a *pulse* . . ."

• • •

At five o'clock I rapped on the door to 406 in the VA building with a tremulous fist.

"C'min."

Whoa. He sat at a draftsman's board made of glass. The top, an inch thick, was the size of a small billiards table. The base was a stupendous nickel-plated mechanism of shimmering gears, cranks, and levers that were ready to be set to the proper coordinates and send the whole thing blasting into orbit. I'd never seen anything like it, before or since. It made me want to kneel before its Machine Age majesty and beg for my Luddite soul. During our entire exchange Winter remained bent over it, engrossed in some-

thing far more interesting than I would ever be.
Me: a pesky satellite.

"Hap."

"Yes."

"I won't have to see anything like that, ever,
again. Will I?"

"N-no, I—"

"Which goes double for anyone else. Clear?"

"Certainly, yo—"

"Fine. Don't slam the door."

So much for my mighty "quotes" shield—it lay
on the floor crumpled and riddled with holes. I
didn't even have the power to ask him what my
grade was. Shit, didn't I deserve better than this
after what we . . .

No, you fool, he was *unconscious*.

At least I still had six more of the Polaroids.

Every angle. Boy, was I going to give *those* a
workout.

I turned to go, and hesitated—the Salvation
Army in me took command: "Mmm, at the risk
of, well, sticking my nose in it, there's something
. . . else I'd like to say."

He finished drawing something. "Speak."

"Well, it's just, about Besti—Mike. I think,
you're a little rough on him. I mean, he actually
works really hard, and—"

"Hap." I braced myself. As he made his declaration, he started to erase something. "The worm
forgives the plow."

End of discussion.

"Right." Well, I tried. "See you at the opening tomorrow?" At last he raised his head.

A terrible smile.

"Wouldn't miss it."

• • •

Turns out the Arts and Architecture Faculty Show, which I so airily dismissed before, was—to a small group of participants—of much graver importance than you could ever tell from just looking at it. It was a hierarchical checklist. A scorecard, for those who knew how to read it—of who ranked where in the School of A & A.

I was later made privy: seniority, tenure, favored-nation status with the dean, all of it played a part in the show's arrangement. The art itself was of less than no importance (Surprise!). Very simple: it was all about where the work was in relation to the entrance to the lobby gallery. The closer you were to the door, the better your position.

Winter's was way, way in the back, around a corner to the left, in a cul-de-sac.

The show opened at six thirty on Friday. Hims and I went at seven.

When we got there, a sense of disquiet socked us from the get-go. Weird: everyone swarmed in the atrium *outside* the gallery, sipping jug wine, munching cheese curds. Dottie, resplendent in mud-colored horizontal wide-wale corduroy, didn't even deign to acknowledge us (her former "protégés"!) as she exchanged gripes and arched eyebrows with Misty and a visiting French quasi-expressio-theorist whom we'd named Bobo.

"What gives?" asked Hims, opening the door to the gallery. "Oh!—"

Yikes. The *smell*. Rotting shit—no other way to describe it. Faint—but unmistakable, and everywhere. Backed-up toilet? We got our glasses of grape-juice-with-a-giggle from the abandoned refreshments table and ventured forward. I pulled out a handkerchief and used it as a gas mask. Hims picked up a few napkins next to the Triscuits and did the same.

Dottie's new body of work lay beyond. She was really taking herself to the next tier. Paintings of: a mounted moose head lying on the floor with an apple in its mouth, *The Last Supper* from the back, and a portrait of what appeared to be Charles Laughton in a blue flannel nightgown and curlers. All second from the front—no dummy *she*.

Winter, the only other person in the gallery, loitered, taking them in. Hands in pockets.

"Hi there," I said. He spun.

Double-breasted worsted wool ash gray suit.

Yellow-on-yellow necktie, its tight Windsor knot like a lighthouse lamp just lit in the twilight blue of his shirt collar. The sails of a matching four-square. Toffee-colored suede wingtips. Groomed. Waiting for Mr. Cukor to call him on set. Supreme.

"Kiddies."

"You *smell* that?"

"Smell *what*? This?" He winked and nodded to Dottie's ka-blooey period.

"Where's yours?" I asked, from under the cotton.

"Follow the yellow brick road." He hiked a thumb to the back.

We went to find it. The further into the gallery, the worse the stench.

"Christ, I hope they called the *custodian*."

"Kind of makes *sense*, actually," said Hims.

It all flowed past us: rough sketches for watercolors of lakeside tree stumps; snow-fogged somethings; a five-point stag, startled and insulted that it had been made into kitsch—**again**; a ceramic cuckoo clock, "hand-painted" and no cuckoo in sight; a series of round placemats, in different sizes, meant to represent the planets; a collection of pennies, pasted onto a rubber mat in the shape of Pennypacker Hall (get it?); and oh, the things that had been done to flowers—asters to zinnias—put in more grotesque poses than virgins in the Book of Martyrs. This *salon* culminated in a succession of nude self-portraits, eight when I stopped counting, by a portly man with inoperable gout and a very open mind, who really, *really* ought to have been turned over to the authorities.

Too many freaks, not enough circuses.

We turned left at the rear, and made it to the Sorbeck Shrine. Four projects.

Mills plotzed. "Cripes, who's teaching *whom?*"

The first was a book cover for *Hitler's Switzerland: The Illusion of Neutrality During the Third Reich* by Joseph Donald McC., and published by Spiral Books. A plain white rectangle seemed to float over a charred, ashen background. The title and author type was set in a Newsprint face that dropped out white from a viscera red band running along the bottom. Offset by the black and white, the scarlet-backed lettering gave just the right hint of the Swiss flag and sprang off the surface. No author could have wished for better.

The second was a poster about war atrocities that he'd offset-lithographed himself, probably because no printer in town would have touched it: a wrenching UPI photograph of a preteen Asian girl with both arms blown off, dazed and lying in the middle of a battle-ravaged street—Nagasaki, probably. Two-hundred point teletype

letters, across the top, spelled out I AM NOT
ARMED. Underneath the picture, in an orange
no-nonsense political campaign poster font:
VOTE NO ON MILITARY EXPENDITURE
BILL #151.

Whatever *that* was.

"Hilarious," Himillsy rasped. "Where's my
design credit?"

The third was another poster. Horizontal.
Smoke stacks—the very same from *Titans of
Industry*, now blown up to truly alarming scale,
threatening to choke the viewer before he could
read it. Slabbed-serif block characters in alter-
nating red, white, and blue bled off the top and
sides.

U.S. STEEL:
KEEPING AMERICA BEAUTIFUL SINCE
1875!

And finally: a white enameled metal box with
rounded corners and edges, resting about three
feet off the ground on a plain black slab pedestal.
I recognized it as the deluxe ice chest from the
window of McClanahan's Sporting Goods, for
the tailgate partymaven who has everything. The
school's logo was appliquéd onto the front in
cloisonné, and it clocked in at a hundred and
fifty smackers. Winter had silkscreened, onto its

lid, in sans-serif Trade Gothic Condensed five-inch high lettering,

WHATEVER YOU DO, DON'T OPEN . . .

Someone already had, and hastily tried to re-seal it.

I asked Hims: "Should I?"

"Go ahead. Hurry up and let's beat it."

I lifted and released a Pandora's worth of reeking horror. A brown lava nightmare of festering poop filled it to the top. More words, on the inside of the lid, in the same style as the others, formed a series of phrases that trailed into the dreadful muck, until they became completely submerged.

THE CURRENT CURRICULUM.
THE ACTING ADMINISTRATION.
CAMPUS ARCHITECTURE.
THE WHOLE GODDAMN LOT OF—

"Shut it! *God!*"

Bam!

Eyes tearing.

"Puke and *barf,* he's gone *borneo!*"

And he was nowhere in sight by the time we got back to the entrance. I practically pulled the door off its hinges. Sweet, sweet air.

On our way to the car, Hims, who'd been auditing French lit that term, said, "Well, now we know."

"What."

"Winter Sorbeck is a madman who thinks he's Winter Sorbeck."

• • •

The Crock of Shit, as it quickly became known, was gone from the gallery by the next morning, but nonetheless became an instant legend in the VA building. Most everyone was scandalized, naturally, but here and there one overheard whispers of admiration—even the muttered admission (from me, at least) that it was "the only piece that mattered." There was no mention of it in the review of the show in Monday's *Collegian*.

Which was glowing, by the way.

• • •

At last: Springtime at State. May-pole dances, Postmidterm depression, Frisbees, the Faculty Show, and of course, Fiji Island.

Phi Gamma Iota was the only fraternity with its house actually on campus—the rest were over the town line. The school wasn't legally supposed to support any "selective societies," so Fiji exercised a loophole and, once a semester, threw open its doors to everyone for a big "house" bash with a vague South Pacific theme, selling tickets to benefit some nameless charity. This allowed it to stay closed the rest of the year. Feege was the Football Frat—at least a third of the brothers were in the gridiron.

I was just going to go by myself—figured it was the only way I'd see the inside of a frat house without having to put my rear up for paddling. I wouldn't even have dreamed of suggesting it to Himillsy, it just sort of slipped out the afternoon of the party. She jumped. "Oh! Let's go together! A kick in the pants! Pick you up at eight."

• • •

Were it not for the Corvair, I wouldn't have recognized her. "Himillsy?"

"No, not tonight! Tonight I'm . . ." she got out of the car and spun like a dervish ". . . Swoozie Moonshoe!"

"The *heck*?"

She was Molecule Monroe, down to the mole, in a voluptuous poofy blonde wig, stuffed ice blue cashmere "headlights" sweater, teeny saddle shoes, and flouncy black poodle skirt. Stunning, really, in a sort of "Marilyn had an abortion but it lived and went on to public school" kind of way.

"And you're . . . Derrick Dick!" She pulled out a bulky State letterman's sweater from the trunk and handed it over.

"I'm *what*?"

"Lose the tie! We're Derrick and Swoozie, the toast of campus! There's not a party blazing that doesn't pray we'll bound through the door and ruin the glamour curve! The gown is our oyster!"

I pulled on the cardigan, which she must have gotten at the Goodwill and embroidered with "Derrick." It made me feel like Tab Hunter's stand-in. And maybe even like . . . her date. "Oh, Swoozie, you're the bee's knees!" I chimed, emboldened by my new role, "you filthy *bitch*!"

Fifteen minutes later we gained the steps of Fiji's fraternal fortress—a horrendous quasi-Athenian pile of columns and flagstone that made Tara look like tract housing. But I'll admit, for this one heady night, I was alive with the thought: we were going to be *included.*

In front of the doors a doughy pledge sat at a card table with a lock box and an ink pad, collecting the cash in exchange for hand stamps. He had extremely bucked teeth.

"That's funny," Miss Moonshoe brayed at him

and handed him a fiver, "*I* don't see a hand up your ass."

"*What?*"

"I always thought Kukla had a hand up his ass."

"Swoozie!" I said, winking at the moose and scared out of my wits and rushing us along, "You minx! You must be *stopped*!"

Luckily we were swallowed by a crowd as thick as he was. I took her elbow.

"Swooze, try not to get Derrick killed before he gets a chance to knock back a few, deal?"

"Oh, I know. That Swoozie, she's such a *shrew*. And a slut! Derrick should drop her like a molten bowling ball."

"We need some sort of secret signal," I offered, "in case we're stuck in a conversation and really want to get going."

"Okay, our secret signal will be, 'Say, let's blow this piss-ridden meat pit.' "

"Fine."

We advanced to the main hall, already aroar with a saturnalia of sozzled gestures and gibbering. The air was a rancid-sock tang of beer—on the breath of all and spilled on the backs of the unsuspecting with clumsy fake apologies. A fleet of aluminum kegs lined the base of each wall, all fitted with acrylic taps stamped with the logo for a brand that could be had for pennies a gallon and was rumored to be brewed purely from Skuylkill River runoff. I stood in line to get us two jars. Suddenly the room went dark and people started chanting in unison.

"Snake! Snake! Snake! Snake! Whoooohoooo!" A spotlight snapped on, focused to a far corner. Claps and cheers, as a penny-pretty blonde got up onto a wooden dinner table and stepped into the glare. Two goons in Fiji sweaters joined her, one holding a rubber hose and a funnel, the other with two glass pitchers of beer. They had everyone's attention. She got on her knees and folded her arms behind her, to wild screams of approval.

"*Snake! Snake! Snake! Snake! Sna—*"

The frantic mantra drove her on, as she threw back her head, closed her eyes, and opened her mouth. The tube was lowered, her lips clutched it, and the hose goon fit the funnel into the other end, which he held up like Miss Liberty's torch. The brew goon, on tiptoe, held the pitchers to either side of the funnel.

"*Snake! Snake! Snake! Snake! Sna—*"

He slowly tilted them symmetrically, producing a steady stream. The tube shuddered and she gave a slight recoil with the first gulp, then opened up her throat to allow for the flow. Her body started to undulate, slightly at first, then building into spasms.

Half the beer to go. No stopping. I found myself chanting along with the crowd. Her nostrils flared to pull in oxygen. A quarter left. She was jerking now, but still in a measure of control. Occasionally it would fill her and leak out the sides of her mouth, but she'd rebound and suck it back up and into her gullet. The slightest flame of teared eyeshadow started to bloom from the edge of each lid.

"Ullk!"

And it was done. Unanimous approval.

"HHHHHHYYYYYAAAAAAAAYYYYYYY!"

She was on all fours, heaving air, trying to hide the panic. Then she sat back on her haunches, eyes closed, and smiled the smile of a drowned corpse. The goons got her to her feet. And the cheering went on for minutes, till the lights and ukulele music came up.

I brought Swoozie her Skuylkill punch. "You catch the floor show?"

"Serves her right, that hosebag." She bolted the brew.

"Hey there, doll, refill?" A towering guy in a Hawaiian shirt whose shining face looked very familiar cocked a pitcher at Swoozie. Oh my God—yes, it was *him.*

"Sure, slugger."

But his pitcher was empty. "Shucks. Be back in a sec. Don't move."

He went to fill it. I was in disbelief.

"Do you know who that *is*?"

"What, that big *jamoke*? Damfino."

"Hims—*Swoozie*, that's *Lacy Rocklins*."

"Who—?"

"The *quarter*back. I thought you read the *Collegian*."

Appalled. "Not the *sports* page."

"Jesus, try the *front* page."

The Lawrence C. Rocklins story had been the multiteated dog that college newspaper stringer-pups just *dream* of sucking from. Despite his modest beginnings (naturally), little Lacy showed great promise on the field from the age of ten. Won a scholarship. Then, in one of those situations that'd seem woefully contrived if you saw it in a movie—as a freshman he was called on to sub for the quarterback (due to an unlikely combination of injury and illness, taking out the first and second stringers) in the squeaker of the year against Georgia Tech. Bagged it in a spectacular thirty-yard bomb with two seconds to go, and has started ever since. He was still only a junior, with his senior year to look forward to, and the pros after that.

It was also reported, more that once, that Lacy was one of identical twins—the other having died in the womb.

"Here ya go. Fill 'er up, Miss—?"

And just looking at him, I knew why: even as a fetus this guy couldn't stand any competition. He filled Swoozie's glass. I held mine up. He ignored it.

"Moonshoe. Swoozie Moonshoe." Flawless straight face, like it was etched on her birth certificate. "And this is my cousin, Derrick."

Gee, thanks a lot.

"I'd have remembered a knockout like you, Swooze," Lacy crooned. "You a transfer?"

Mr. Smoothie. *Please.* Hims didn't disappoint.

"Oh, Lucy, are you out of your *tits?* I go to Babson."

"Lacy." He was caught off guard, probably for the first time in three seasons. "R-really. Gosh . . . do you know Casey Carmichael?"

Mills nodded at the name. "*Know* her. God, we practically have the same spit."

"Wow. She's swell. Is she really pinned to a Beta?"

"A Beta?"

"Beta Theta Pi?"

"Nah. Apple Brown Betty, actually."

He tried to place it. "Hmm. Do they have a chapter here?" Not joking.

"Um," she bit back a smirk. "Beats me. Actually, it's funny you asked about her. Isn't it a *shame?*" She became serious.

"What?"

Whoever Casey was, I felt sorry for her already.

"Oh. Never mind. Thought you heard."

"Aw, don't leave me hanging, I won't tell. Casey's a great gal, I think the world of her."

"Well, you're not alone on *that* score."

"Oh?"

"Last weekend . . . oh, I really shouldn't."

"Swooze, please?" Amazing. She was making the BMOC into her pinky ring.

"Oh, all right . . . but you did NOT hear it from *me*."

"Scouts." He held up his right hand.

"Well." We huddled. Thrilling. Lacy, Derrick, and Swoozie: the State center of the universe. "It seems that Case had to be . . . rushed, to Emergency."

"No soap! Is she all right?"

"Well, she is *now*. But they had to pump her stomach."

"Drink too much?"

"Yes, actually. But not . . . hootch."

"No? What then?"

"Now remember, you dragged this out of me . . ." She gave it her coquettish best. "Jism. At least a pint."

Lacy reared in shock.

"And it wasn't just one—"

"Pardon—" He turned and bolted for the kegs.

I leaned into her. "Swooze, ease *up*."

"Derrick, can I help it if Casey Carmichael is just a bouncing, bubbly bed bauble?" She drained her jar and signaled for more. I obliged.

"So Swooze," I asked, when I got back, "whaddaya think Winter's gonna lay on Hap and Girleeny for the final crit?"

She sighed. "Oh, he'll probably go easy on 'em, like 'redo the Sistine Chapel ceiling with me as God', or 'design a hangar big enough for my ego.' Something simple."

After ten or so minutes, Lacy came back.

"Hey, Swoozie, you up for a kick?"

"Sure."

He motioned for us to follow. We went out of the main hall and turned into a small brick passageway. A left, and then fifty feet to an oak door. Lacy pounded three times—once, a beat, then twice. It creaked open. The din of another party leaked out. We descended steps, sort of down to a Skeller within the frat house. Fascinating. A full service bar down here. Pledges darted about, stepping and fetching for the brothers—some at tables, playing cards and quarters; others leaning on the bar issuing casual demands. Lacy asked us our pleasure.

"Martinis," Swoozie chimed, and that's when I noticed, with not a little unease: she was the only girl here.

She lit a cig and met all the stares with, "What's the matter? Never seen a *skirt* before?" A few chuckles, a few sneers.

Not in here, Miss Moonshoe.

A nervous pledge came up to me with a fat roll of ones and started to take bets.

"What'll ya have? Three or three-ten. Rest are taken."

"For what?"

He looked at me as the tourist I was.

"The bluck chug."

Vermont had taught me the term when he was rushing AGR. Bluck: the noisome effluvia that collects on a frat's basement floor—a combination of spilt beer, grime, puke, and piss. My eyes strained in the stale light, to gutters that ringed the room, which caught and drained it into a single shoe box–sized basin in one of the corners. By eleven-thirty it was a good six inches deep.

"Th-three." I handed him two bucks. "Um, three, what, actually?"

"Minutes, squid." He handed me a little red carnival ticket with the number on it and left for the next brother, muttering, "... three-ten left ..."

Lacy started tapping on a glass with a spoon. Soon all the brothers joined in. The pledges put down whatever they were doing and gathered in the center of the room. Playing cards were dealt to each of them and affixed with tape to their foreheads. They all looked as if they were waiting for biopsy results.

Lacy presented Swoozie with a deck and bowed. "Doll, you may have the honors."

"Cut it?" she asked. He nodded. She picked up half the stack.

"Four of clubs." Looks all around. No one had it.

"Try again."

"Ace of hearts."

Shouts, as a boy with the matching card on his face wobbled forward, accompanied by a brother holding a stopwatch. Beads of sweat sprouted on his temples. Lacy went over to the bluck drain, dipped a large shotglass into it, and hoisted it up—full to the brim. It looked like molasses and smelled just the opposite.

Ace of hearts, terrified, took it from him, his trembling hand threatening to lose it.

"Skizzy, you ready?" asked Lacy.

"Check," grinned the stopwatch goon.

"Okay, on the count of three . . ."

"*One!*" the brothers wailed in unison.

Ace shut his eyes.

"*Two!*"

And closed his nose.

"*Three!!*"

And, yeek, filled his mouth. His bottom lip shook violently, ready to jettison all of it.

"You spit it out, you drink two," said Lacy, calm but firm, like a mother with a sick child who doesn't want his Vicks. Ace squeezed his eyes tighter and downed it in one greasy gulp. He lifted the empty glass and Skizzy started the timer.

"Ten seconds . . . twenty . . . "

Ace's peepers opened.

". . . thirty . . . forty . . ."

And bulged.

". . . fifty . . . one minute . . ."

His torso: in peril. Quaking.

". . . seventy seconds . . ."

Gasping. Ready to burst.

"In the trough, Einstein, in the TROUGH." Lacy snapped.

He just made it to the bluck basin before erupting in a wet explosion that sounded like a giant pig falling to its death. Then he passed out.

"Eighty seconds." Skizzy clicked the button.

"Yeah," Lacy said, lazily. "You never buy bluck, you only rent it."

"A minute twenty!" roared a letter-sweatered Neanderthal the size of a DeSoto with four leis around his neck and a beer stein in the shape of half a football in each hand. "I win!"

Swoozie looked at them all like a microbiolo-
gist observing malignant germs on a slide.

Then the barking started.

A three-hundred-pound, seven-foot-tall Sal
Mineo just started howling like a Saint Bernard
in heat. Another joined him, and then everybody
did. Swooze gaped at me in wonderment—
astray in hell's kennel. Something, skittering
across the floor, bumped into my leg and headed
for the middle of the room, joining the others—
the pledges, on all fours. Dogs, screaming, paw-
ing the cobblestone floor.

"Alright," Lacy declared, quieting them down.
They sat like adoring pets and waited for
instruction. "Who has a joke? Someone, amuse
me."

"I do, sir," panted a stocky, black-haired guy
with a unibrow and a neck as thick as an oak
stump.

"Okay, you. If it makes me laugh, you may get
up."

"Yessir." He cleared his throat. "W-why didn't
the niggers mind when their baby was still-
born?"

"Dunno."

"At least they knew where their next meal was
coming from."

Jesus.

Lacy broke up, as did everybody else—Derrick and Swoozie excepted. "Alright, good job, Tinky." The lummox stood.

"Me next, sir?" said another dog-boy, with red hair and freckles—an Irish setter? Lacy nodded to him.

"Why'd they bury the nigger in a turtleneck?" asked Irish.

"I'll bite."

"To hide the rope burn!"

A real yuckfest. A nice pat on the head for Irish.

Swoozie threw her cig on the floor and crushed it. She looked, as she would put it, *miles* south of charmed.

"Hey, LUCE!" She yelled, and a startled hush descended—she had the floor. "I heard a real oner the other day."

Lacy: bemused. "Yeah?"

"Yeah. How many football players does it take to screw in a lightbulb?"

His face: a dark question mark. Didn't answer.

"Six. They each get three credits for it and *still* end up screwing each other by mistake!"

Angry silence, everywhere. Then hisses. This was not good. I whispered hotly into her ear.

"Himillsy, that's the *limit.* Let's blow this piss-ridden meat pit, when I get back from the can, I mean it!"

"*After* we get our drinks."

I went to the john, off of one corner, and holed up in a booth. Just as I was wiping, two people barged in and I heard a familiar voice.

"-king bitch. Teach *her*. Hell with her *cousin* . . . "

I finished and put my eye to the gap between the door and the jamb.

"That it? Swell." Could just make it out: A Feege goon and . . . Lacy, pouring a fine white powder into a martini glass. Stirred. The door squeaked and I couldn't see them anymore. I put my head to the floor—no feet.

I slipped out of the loo, cracking the door onto the main room of the cellar and easing myself out. Oh, no—Lacy was talking to Swooze, who swilled, slurped . . . and swooned. Into his arms.

Animal cheers.

Lacy: heading up the stairs. Carrying Hims.

No. *No.*

Me: hopeless, helpless. Impossible to follow them—they'd all be on me like mush-huskies with a pork chop.

My heart: destroying itself.

I slid against the wall, looking for an escape route. None. No fire exit, or any other way out. Something scraped across my back. I turned—a knob. A row of knobs. Not labeled, but they had to be . . .

I studied them, then the path to the steps.

Closed my eyes to memorize it, opened them, and in a single stroke, turned all the switches to Off.

Nightfall.

Made a break for it, pushing through the pitch bluck black, the air stolen to the hoots and shrieks of the lout menagerie, which pawed at me and fought itself in the dark, in the hot beer breath. Someone grabbed my arm. I thrashed and wriggled out of the sweater and kept going. I found the stairs, and charged for the door. Just through it, the lights came back on.

Into the passageway. No one in sight. Foot-steps, shouts, behind me.

The main hall. I struggled through gaggles of Fiji Islanders to lose the dogs and get to the grand staircase. At the top: Lacy and his prize, leaving the balcony. I bounded up the steps and into a hall of suites, just in time to see the door to Lacy's pull shut, the lock clicked.

Shit!

Think, *think*. It worked in the basement—maybe if I found the main power switch for the whole place, I could . . . forget it. Take too long.

And . . . no, not the lights, the . . . yes!

Racing like a madman. Whereisitwhereisit. Has to has to be here. No luck . . . but weren't they required by law on all campus buildings? Came to a door marked UTILITY CLOSET.

Pulled it open. Yes! Sweet Jesus: a red Bakelite unit, on the far wall, in the dark. I pulled the ceiling bulb's ball-bearing cord to read it.

IN CASE OF EMERGENCY
BREAK GLASS

With what? Pounded. Cracks. Got out my dorm keys. Made them into brass knuckles.

Crick! Crick! Hurry! He could be . . . no don't think it, don't think it pull at the glass, the metal handle. Jerked it.

CLLLLLLLLLLLLLAAAAAAAAANNNNNGG!

The sprinklers went off. Somewhere people started shouting.

I sprang from the closet and screamed my lungs out, running, banging on doors. "Fire! FIRE! Everybody OUT!" Beat on Lacy's. "Lace! Lace! Fire! Hup TO buddy!" I ran around the corner and hid so I could see his door. Come *on*, you big jamoke. And please be *alone* . . .

It popped open a moment later. The fair-haired Frankenstein was furiously tucking his shirt back in his pants. Muttering vague profanity, he shielded his face against the sprinklers and went down the hall to investigate. When the coast was clear, I bolted into the room.

She was lying on the lower bunk, still Swoozie. Out cold. I yanked off the wig, threw it out the window, and put her arms around my neck. Lifted.

Into the hallway. Pandemonium. People running now, every which way, including me. From the balcony I looked down onto a soggy, orderless glob of havoc. I turned and made for the other end of the hall through the spray. Followed two brothers to a back stairwell. Down it. Tried two doors. Wouldn't budge. Another flight of steps to a third, which opened, onto . . . the lawn.

On a trip to the zoo when I was seven, my cousin and I were presented with the opportunity to hold in our very own hands a large and supposedly harmless African tarantula. My response was to pass out immediately. But Jay, two years older and never known to shy away from anything that held the possibility of total catastrophe, practically grabbed it. When I came to, I asked him what it was like. His response was uncharacteristically thoughtful:

"Two things surprised me," he said. "It had heat. And it had weight."

I practically fainted again.

And so it was actually to carry Himillsy, whom I'd never so much as dared touch. Her mantle may have provided the illusion of a bloodless invertebrate, but not so—actual physical warmth rose from her rag doll frame.

I was darting across the grass, from the chaotic back drop. Towards the car. Where did we *park*?

"Himillsy! Wake up!"

"Whuuuu . . . "

Finally found it. I propped her gently against the door.

"Wake up! We've got to get out of here! Now!" I rattled her.

"G-Garnett?"

"No, it's me! Himillsy, listen! You've been drugged. I don't know where your car keys are!"

She shook her head as if she'd just surfaced from a dive. Started laughing.

Then stopped, angry. Realized it was me. "What the Hell are YOU doing?"

What? "Getting us the hell out of Dodge, if that's all right. Didn't think you wanted to be *raped* just now, sorry."

"I was having FUN! You had no right to stop it! What're *you*, my chaperone?" She sneered. "My *hero*?"

How DARE she? "I thought I was your friend! Jesus Goddamned Christ! Do you have any idea what kind of a spot I just got you out of?" I was in burning disbelief. "At least Winter *seemed* grateful."

"*Win*ter?" She was totally disgusted. "Jesus, if you could only see yourself in class, sitting there staring at him . . ."

"Stop it."

". . . hanging on every word . . . with your mouth wide open. Sickening."

How could she? I backed away. "At least . . ." I grasped for it, "*he* has something to *say*." This got what I wanted—her hurt and fury. God, how did it all collapse into *this*, so quickly?

She ran up to me, still unsteady from her Mickey Finn. "You mean someone to fire at!" She lost herself to hysterics, "You don't *get* it! We are the fish! In his barrel!"

I replied, with sick calm, "No. *You* are the cat, in his bag." She shouldn't have known what that meant, but she obviously did—it must have been the way I said it. I'd clearly crossed the line.

Ballistic. "And you! Love him!"

Please . . . please don't become my enemy. "Enough." Because I will destroy you.

"You . . . LOVE him." She was figuring it out, as always. No . . . "You love him THAT! WAY!"

Had we been in a movie, this would be where I'd have slapped her. I didn't dare, because it wouldn't have been just a slap—I'd have kept going until she was a red, wet spot on the grass. So I did something else.

I'd become pretty good at figuring things out too.

I looked over, towards the car. "And who do *you* love? Anyone?"

"No!—"

I was there in a single motion. Hand in the glove compartment. Pulled him out.

"Any . . . *thing?*"

She was powerless to move.

Aloft, my sacrifice. My hands on the head and shoulders, poised to open him like a fleshy bottle of Crush. I started twisting, testing. Wouldn't be easy.

That was okay, I had all night.

Polyurethane is strong. My human terror, and longing, and tortured frustration and my heart—full of the worst kind of love—were stronger. I yanked and strained and regripped and pulled again.

She stared—petrified, incredulous.

And then it wasn't Baby Laveen anymore, it was *me*: the spawn of Himillsy and Winter who can only watch and admire with eyes wide open, who polishes the apples only to have them cored and quartered, consumed and . . . disposed of. This was a mirror I couldn't bear to look into anymore. And I would dispose of *it*.

Finally a crack in the rubber neck and a little plea popped from the rear of the upper mezzanine in my head.

"Please, don't."

Too late. The last pink strand stretched and gave with a recoiling *SNAP!*

His head in my left fist.

I wound up and sent it into space. Landed somewhere with a small leaf splash in the Fiji hedges. Tossed the body into the passenger seat of the car.

Then something much more than a scream and much less than human flew out of her and before I knew it she was gunning the engine.

The car leapt onto the sidewalk, did a doughnut on the lawn, hesitated, and shot to the road.

Yes, go. Good. I'm . . . good.

And I am dead.

• • •

She didn't show up for Winter's penultimate class, two days later. I wasn't surprised. I barely made it there myself—the events had been so desolating, I sent them into exile just so I could get out of bed. As we waited for the last assignment, I saw there were nine of us left.

Ideal.

Winter didn't comment one way or the other and was especially brusque and subdued as he gave us our instructions. "For the final critique, it's very simple. I want you to look back on the four core projects, and combine them into one—taking into account all you've seen and heard here. It can take any form that you prefer, but remember, as in the 'word' problem, examine the content very, very carefully before deciding how it's going to look. Let the one inform the other. And it better . . ." He looked through us, to something impossible, ". . . astonish me." Didn't even bother to light up.

"That's all."

Himillsy, for all intents and purposes, had vanished. There was no way to directly contact her room, and I wasn't even sure I wanted to—goddamnit, she could make the effort this time.

But true to form, I started to come around from the whole thing and kidded myself I hadn't done anything too terrible—it was the booze. She'd cool off eventually. She always did.

All that high drama, over a doll. Ridiculous.

I at least wanted to get her the final crit assignment, so I loitered across the street from Garnett's apartment that afternoon, hoping to "run in" to her. To kill the time I worked out in my head what my final project would be . . .

There was an old Vandercook letterpress proofing machine and dozens of wood and lead type trays that ended up in the Belly when a local type foundry folded in the wake of the onset of photolettering technology. The Lithography TA had showed me how to use it. And now I would—to make a series of six broadsides based on notes I had taken all semester. Using just large type and stark backgrounds, they would be recruitment posters for the class, using slogans culled from Winter—the course name and number would appear, small, at the bottom of each one.

From the first day:
> THAT WAS LOUSY. DO IT AGAIN.

From the first critique:
> THIS ISN'T A CLASSROOM,
> IT'S AN ARENA.

From the second:
> LIMITS ARE POSSIBILITIES.

From the third:
> GOOD IS DEAD.

From the fourth:
> DON'T LOOK NOW!

And finally,
> ASTONISH ME.

I'd construct a cloth-bound portfolio case for them, with a label. What to call it? What would Himillsy call it? Something weird, enigmatic . . . like Barnum's "This Way to the Egress." Of course:

THE CHEESE MONKEYS

By dusk I'd had no luck and couldn't afford to wait any longer. I trudged over to her dormitory.

I left the final's instructions—in an envelope, Himillsy's name scrawled on it—with the building's desk monitor.

. . .

Friday morning. Mike, Maybelle, and I set up camp in the Belly of the VA building, figuring we could pool our resources, even if they just amounted to peerage coaxing. We had until Tuesday afternoon to distill twelve weeks of work into a single heady dram, a coherent whole—in addition to preparing for our other finals. I felt cheated that Himillsy had deserted us (or more specifically, *me*), and was furious with her anew while simultaneously hoping she'd burst in on us any minute and stake her claim, so all could be forgiven.

Crenck and Mabes discussed their plans, but I stayed vague about mine. Mike's approach was to do the word "volatile" in matches, make an identity look like a hitchhiking sign, and paint a "Keep America Beautiful" poster using smoke stacks which somehow become the stripes in the American flag. I finally decided to flat-out tell him.

"Look. That's not going to cut it."

"How come?"

"Well, for one thing, it's three separate projects, not one."

"Oh."

"You have to *consolidate* them. Weren't you listening?" You worm.

"Oh. How?"

"That's the question, exactly, we all have to figure it out."

Maybelle was claiming an entire table with her art supplies. "Mine's going to be a big jigsaw puzzle, and when you put it together, it'll make a calligraphied sign that sends out an SOS using carnival colors."

For her, that was an atomic mental breakthrough.

"Good for you."

I'd already pulled an "all-nighter" or two last semester, but this was going to be different. I sat down and made a list of everything that had to get done by Tuesday afternoon, and figured I could just finish it all in time.

Provided I didn't sleep. I mean really—not a wink.

Mike and Maybelle came to the same conclusion. Had we any idea what we were in for, we'd never have tried it.

Winter would have wanted me to tell it this way: The first day, the hard realities are just theory—the deadline is still abstract and you're not in a rush. You laugh, you're at ease, you work slowly—as if extra time can be delivered on demand at some point, like a pizza. You stay calm.

And later you will regret it, deeply.

But for now, one day turns into the next, and you don't notice too much out of the ordinary. You've got a job to do, and the weight of the requirements begins to tug accordingly. But hey—no windows, mercifully, in the Belly. Just a long night's journey into day. What time is it?

At forty-eight hours, it's the hardest—the clock has decided who's the rodent in its wheel and you're not running fast enough. You fret, you're going to collapse, and . . . you don't quit. It's weird. You keep thinking, "I really have to shut down, any minute," and you're going to, just as soon as you have the second page up and running. Though after that, oh shit, ink the press up for the third, before stopping, and then it's . . .

The third day. You're under the rainbow and the spotlight of the Divine Tragic Absurd shines its black light everywhere and helps you grow like a mushroom. You sharpen a pencil and it's just the saddest thing since the Creation. You verge on weeping—in silent isolation—for five minutes. Then the point snaps against your work top and it puts you into fits of hysteria. Wipe your eyes and proceed. You foolishly take a break and emerge to street level. Mars. Make it to the Caf, to refuel, and you're seeing it for the first time because you realize everyone *acts* as if they have no idea you've been awake for over seventy-two hours, but they've *known* all along and can barely contain their horror and admiration. You are fortified and ashamed. You have three helpings of mashed potatoes (so easy to *chew!*) and a half a glass of Coke. You take an apple and a banana for later, leave them on your tray, and toss them into the garbage as you leave.

When you realize this, halfway back to the VA building, you find the nearest curb and sit. Eyes moist. Innocent fruit—they deserved better.

So alone.

• • •

After ninety-six hours, it's not a pencil anymore, it's a yellow pointypointy that makes marks for you when you give it brain signals and frankly it's bored and wants a life of its own. Can you blame it? Of course you can. Someone made it. How did they get the hard blackyblack in there? Was it Space Beings? The pointypointy drops yellow to the floor. The floor is fifty feet down. You'll drown if you go after it. No more pointypointy. A pen, yes, get a pen. Yes. It would feel clean and good in your hand, if your fingers weren't numb. No blackyblack in it. Bluesygoo.

How'd bluesygoo get *in* there?

Then your mother bursts through the door in a giant silver wig and a see-thru muumuu, carrying the biggest beach ball you've ever seen. It's decorated to look like the world and she just keeps bouncing it and bouncing it, singing, "*Una paloma blanca . . .*"

"*Stop* that," you say, and she vanishes.

"Stop what?" Maybelle at the table behind me, startled awake, puzzle pieces stuck to her hair. She was even closer to completion than I was—her "artwork" was done and all she had to do was finish cutting it all up. I still had to glue the portfolio binding and trim my pages. At least they came out half decent.

"Nothing. Sorry."

"Must have dozed. Back to work . . ."

The most cruelly ironic thing about all of it is that your faculties deplete inversely to the rate you need them most. One small slip—a renegade elbow to an open ink pot, a letterpress-printed label (four hours of work) trimmed to the wrong size, spells doom. As your project nears completion, it is becoming more coherent and realized, while you are deteriorating.

Mike, by the way, bore none of the scars of this marathon—he didn't look unshaven because he already had a beard (to cover up the salami skin pallor of his cheeks), and his uncluttered mind was on autopilot. He was a little ripe from where I sat, but that was it. Working away.

I thought: "Someone ought to take the key out of his back." He'd slipped out to get more Cokes when—huh?

Something small, warm, and wet on the back of my neck. Were the pipes leaking? Christ, all we need. Didn't have time to move my tools. Did my tools love me? Wiped it away and looked at my hand. Red ink on my fingers. Red ink? I turned around to ask Mabes if she—

Good. God.

She hadn't even noticed. Eyes barely open. Awake. For a week—the feeling gone from her hands. She was working. She was cutting up all the pieces. So He could put them all back together. Had to get it done.

"Mmmaybelle."

It was all over her.

"What."

"Give. Me, the."

"Ten more minutes, at most." She wiped her brow, she wiped it all over her forehead. "Dear, I need a, a shower."

"X-Acto knife. Put it down." So close, so. Too good. To be true. Of *course* this happens. This *had* to happen.

"Why?" Finally looked up. At herself. "Oh. Oh." A vein. Must have hit a vein. I stood for the first time in hours, to go to her. Wading through lava: at least my legs had slept.

She was too tired to cry. Just stared. Waved her left hand away from her in a wide, lazy arc to banish it from her sight and sent a crescent spray of blood across the tables.

Any on my project, Miss Lee, and I'll kill kill kill you.

The X-Acto leapt from her right hand, missed my foot by less than an inch, and landed blade first into the linoleum. Sagged with a sigh to the floor. "No . . ."

"It's alright." I was . . . trying to get to her hand. God, her hand. I spotted . . . a small dome of red clay on the table in front of her. Clay?

"No . . ."

Her thumb. Tip of her thumb. That she'd sliced off. I needed to get that. She'd want that. Someone get some ice. I'll get that, I thought, just a sec.

Clutched the arm. "Keep it *up*. I'll get a . . . "

Spinning.

"Hold it up." A backwards waltz, she shaking towards me. No, *I* lead. Dip. Up again. No, *up*. Losing our—onto the floor. Laughing. Funniest thing in the world. Tears. Ride it out. Catch breath. Okay. Up, we, go.

"HUHhuhHUHhuhHUHhuh—"

Sat her down. Clean rags in her bag. Picked

up the, urrgh, thumb piece . . . a gum drop (A-plus for D Squared!). Wrapped it, and into my shirt pocket. Wrapped her finger in tissue. Rubber bands. Mike nowhere in sight, Son of a *Bitch*.

Had to get it reattached, pronto, she ever wanted it back. Simply no other option. God, God, damn. I made myself say it. "Let's . . . get to the infirmary."

"It's okay. Go by myself." She waved the bloody stump at me. "Get yours done."

Yes: Mine. Done. All I wanted. So close. I was so . . . happy (heh) with how it was . . . going. Another hour and a half, two, tops. I'd just make it. With time for a shower. Show *him*.

Show *her*. Wherever she was.

Offer again. Have to. "Non. Sense. Let's go."

"No, I . . ." And she was into my arms, blubbering. Twenty-seventh catharsis in the last five days. The blood, the tears, the despair, the smell, the glue, the utter *chasm* of talent, the preposterous hair.

I hated her more than I had ever hated anyone or thing that had dared draw breath.

"Let's. *Go*."

• • •

Took *hours*. Forms. Permissions. Liabilities. Insurance papers. More insurance papers (could

I hand these in as my final project? Oh *God*, I needed sleep). Handing over the exiled thumb tip. Was I sure it was hers? Was there foul play involved?

"Not the kind you're thinking of."

I'd left a quick note in the Belly to Mike, telling him what happened. Now I wondered what it said. Mabelle was led away through swinging white doors, while I handled the paperwork.

I parked myself in the waiting room and between filling in the blanks I tortured myself every two seconds with thoughts like: "I could be gluing on the label right now. I could be doing the final page trimming. I could be wrapping it in acetate to keep it clean . . . "

"Sign here, please."

Scariest of all, I heard my voice say to the head nurse, as I moved the pen up and down: "We have a two-twenty-five final. Mandatory attendance."

I handed in the papers and actually thought of just fleeing, but she made sure I would be escorting Miss Lee home.

"Ssssure."

Home? Not exactly.

I went back to the waiting room, defeated. The torturing recommenced—not from myself, but from a unseen, ugly jury.

Who are you kidding? You wanted, NEEDED this to happen and you know it—you can't believe your luck! You can't bear to finish anything—it's death! If she hadn't done it to herself, you would have had to—

"Shhh . . ."

He'll destroy you. As you destroyed Himillsy.

"Shut *up*."

Stares everywhere—horrified pity for an escapee from a botched firing squad. Don't worry, folks—I'll go back. Wouldn't *miss* it.

Yet another indignity: tried to sleep, couldn't. I read magazines that were printed in dancing hieroglyphics, pictures turned on their heads and back again, laughing at me, asking me questions no one should ever have to answer. It would have been fascinating had it not made me want to scream. A jagged hour passed.

"Hi."

They finally released her at two o'clock. Not even time to go to the Belly and gather our stuff.

Looked as if they'd grafted an oven-mitt onto her arm, hung it from her neck.

". . . hurt?" I asked.

"No. Got to keep it raised. A week. Should take."

"Let's get to class. Just make it."

Solemn. "W-what. Are we going to do . . ." Wretched. ". . . say to him?"

We opened the door onto the poisoned apple of the world.

Feet moving. Heavy, awful steps.

"Don't . . .

. . . know."

BASIC INTER—

We've only discussed, so far, formal matters. Left to Right, Top to Bottom, Big and Small, In Front Of and In Back Of—these are important, certainly, but they only deal with Form: how something looks. Now, as to—

Oh, but look at the time.

We have been talking about Form because, well, we had to start somewhere.
Next time, we'll get into Content.

*Now **that's** where the real **fun** begins . . .*

THE FINAL EXAM.

Art 127 (Introduction to Graphic Design),
Winter Sorbeck, instr.

For which we are required to combine each of the
assignments of the spring semester in order to fashion
from them a pleasing whole.

Too tired to sleep, to care, to fear. Let him do
his worst. Beat me to death and save me the
trouble. I mounted the stairwell in the Baxter
building—might as well have been scaling
Luxor. Opened the door to the hallway, leading
to my . . . tomb.

I was just going to calmly explain what happened. I'd just say I've . . . failed. I've only, ever,
failed.

"I think you should go in."

At the other end, sitting on the bench, in her Fruit Salad Surgery dress, swinging her legs. Her face a Cheshire grin. I . . . reached out to her.

"Hims, it's so great to, I'm . . . sorry."

Gone. Into the air. But she was right. I walked towards where she was sitting. Nothing.

Then I went for the door.

"You can't, it's only a quarter after." Maybelle plodded, delirious, ten paces back. Over on the other bench, actually there: Mike and the others, projects in hand. Waiting. No Himillsy, real or imagined.

"What's he gonna do, throw me out?" I muttered. "Too late for that."

I pushed through, into the room.

No Winter either. Not here yet. Hah.

Just a manila envelope taped to the wall. A note on it—typed on A&A letterhead.

Made my way up. Could barely see:

Kiddies:

It would appear The Cookie Cutters didn't take too kindly to my little installation at the Dog and Pony Show. (Philistines!) As a result, it seems my services here are no longer required. I would have seen out the term, but the June job market looms, and I wanted to get the jump on all of you. I've left your grading slips here, presigned by

yours truly, as a small consolation prize.
You are welcome to fill them out as you see
fit and submit them for processing. I urge
you to be fair.
                                    —W.S.

No. No.

Yes.

I went back to the hallway. "Come on in. Won't believe it."

. . .

David David read it next. "That's too bad. He had potential." He laid the paper on the table and looked for his grading slip. "And he owed me thirty bucks . . ."

Maybelle, who had every right to make the sound of one hand clapping, took in the letter and mumbled "No. He . . . they . . . can't do this." Crushed. "It's not *fair*."

"What? Where is he?" Mike's turn. "When's he coming?" He read it again.

"Well, so much for that," said David David. "Later." He stooped to gather his things from the table.

"No. No one's going anywhere." Mike closed the door. Locked it. Faced us. "We have to grade each other. He *said*. That's how it works . . ."

So much for my impression that Crenck escaped the dementia of sleep deprivation. He crouched like a skinny ogre guarding a bridge and held his X-Acto blade dagger style.

"Mike," I wheezed, "there's no need for—"

"SHUT UP!"

Never seen him like this—breathing crazily.

"Do MINE!" He lifted his project, all four pieces, with one hand—his tray of labor. His rectangular soul. "TELL ME!"

Thick silence.

"I," I started, then the tears—they just . . . *grew* out of me . . . vines trailing down my cheeks and neck and below because . . . I was on the side of the road again, in the middle of nowhere, only this time no message . . . on any piece of paper, no matter what it said, or what it looked like, could ever, ever save me. Winter . . . Hims. You're really gone, aren't you?

And it was all a joke.

God had withdrawn from His creation. A day early.

"Say," said David David, nodding to someone he could see down the hall. "Look, there he is, after all. It's Winter."

I bolted up.

Mike spun like a top. "Where?"

DD hauled off and gave him a good pasting, square across the jaw. Who'd have thought he had it in him? Mike was sprawled on the floor, a hole in his back where the key used to be.

I got to my feet and howled, stepping in front of Crenck's crumpled form. "Hey hey HEY! Don't hurt him!" The minibreakdown had jump-started my batteries. Things regained at least a quasi-clarity they hadn't in days. "He hasn't slept for a week, he doesn't even know his own name . . . for Chris*sakes*."

A knock at the door. In the window: Not Winter, but a guy dressed as a mailman from central casting. God had sent Mercury's flunky. I reached over and unlocked it.

"UPS delivery. Can somebody sign?" He was ready to relieve himself of a considerable burden. I looked at his nametag: PHIL.

Fill. Filled out. "I will, Phil." Did.

Then, a jangling sound. My imagination? No, in the hallway—the pay phone was ringing. I . . . needed to get that. I knew I did. Maybe it was Him. God checking in on his package to Earth.

"Mike," I said slowly, stepping carefully over his crumpled form, "it's the phone. I think . . . I should answer the phone. Right?" He hugged his head and rolled onto his side, sobbing. I went into the hall and picked up the receiver. "Hell—"

"Did it GET there?" Through static: part

desperate plea, part belly laugh, part horror shriek.

It was really *her*. Christ, what had I done to her? "Himillsy!!" I practically jumped through the mouthpiece. "Where are you? I'm *sor–*"

"Is it THERE?"

I could see Phil through the doorway. He carefully put a good-sized box on the table in the center—she'd sent it? Of course. "Yes, it's here. Wh–"

"Is *he* there?"

Phil took a slip of paper from his shirt pocket, studied it a moment, put it back, and slit the box open.

She didn't mean Phil. "Yes," I lied. Why was I lying, why did I care? Because it was her, it was really *her*. And she wanted him here.

And so did I.

"He's here, yes, Winter's here, he–"

"I want him to LOOK AT IT." Phil huffed and lifted it out and set it next to the box as gingerly as he could. It must have weighed a ton. "IS HE LOOKING at it?!!" She was slipping into some-one else—a dissolving acid negative of whoever I thought she was. I could feel her evaporating, with each word.

Oh Jesus—Hims, I'll help you out of this, I swear—I just have to keep you on the line, and find out where you are—"Yes, he's looking at it.

In, in fact, he's smiling." Please. Please don't. I can't let you go again. I'll make it up to you. "Where *are* you? I'll come get y—"

"HaHAH!! Look! It's my final."

In front of Phil was a large glass bowl—two, maybe three feet in diameter. Filled with water and . . . I could just make it out—a tiny, opalescent fish, which zagged and zigged in an iridescent vortex, terrified.

Phil made himself scarce. Everyone descended on it, crowding to get a look. Did they see what I saw? Did they see that she'd aced it, in this single elegant gesture?

From the first crit:
The bowl, relative to the fish, is Kimbrobdagian.

From the second:
The fish has no arms.

From the third:
It can't park anywhere.

And the fourth:
Looks just like a bullet.

Did they want what I wanted?

Did they want to understand, to unlock it? To decode it? To glean, to touch, to learn, to get something, to proceed, to get somewhere, to graduate, to work, to thrive; to someday, sometime, finally earn the luxury, the permission to . . . stop, to *stop* all of this, to relax, and forget?

"Are *YOU* looking at it?" Voice ghostly now.

"Yes, I am. It's . . . brilliant, it is." What does she want to hear? "It's just genius. Now will you *PLEASE* tell me where you *ARE*–"

"You IDIOT." She spent the last of herself. A cinder, a falling firework, "You don't GET IT. I'm in the BOWL! Where I've ALWAYS BEEN!!"

It was as if she'd put the receiver on a table and was backing away from it, screaming but fainter. She'd never retreated from anything, not her.

"What?! Himillsy, I can't see you!" Oh God, I can't *see* you.

"There! That's MMMMEEEEEEEEEEEEEEE–"

Click.

"I want you to design a moment in time. What does that mean? That's what you will show me. At some point this semester (pick a point, any point), you will take something you have made and use it to claim a moment for yourself—yours and only yours—in front of the class. It could be a word, a picture, a poster, a combination of these, hell . . . maybe even a book—you get the idea.

"At least you'd better. Like it or not, you'll be doing it the rest of your life. Might as well put some thought into it.

"And you **will** be graded.

"Ready?

"Go."